5701

BOOKS BY BARBARA CORCORAN

A Dance to Still Music
The Long Journey
Meet Me at Tamerlaine's Tomb
A Row of Tigers
Sasha, My Friend
A Trick of Light
The Winds of Time
All the Summer Voices
The Clown
Don't Slam the Door When You Go
Sam
This Is a Recording
Axe-Time, Sword-Time
Cabin in the Sky
The Faraway Island

The
Faraway Island

The
Faraway Island

by Barbara Corcoran

ATHENEUM · 1977 · New York

Library of Congress Cataloging in Publication Data

Corcoran, Barbara.
The faraway island.

SUMMARY: Arriving on Nantucket Island for a year
with her grandmother, Lynn finds herself faced with
problems of her grandmother's age, "tough kids" at
school, and her own lack of self-confidence.
[1. Grandmothers—Fiction.   2. Nantucket, Mass.—
Fiction]   I. Title.
PZ7.C814Far   [Fic]   76-25152
ISBN 0-689-30550-8

Published simultaneously in Canada by
McClelland & Stewart, Ltd.
Manufactured in the United States of America by
Fairfield Graphics, Fairfield, Pennsylvania
Designed by Mary M. Ahern
First Edition

To Cappy Lambeth Carlton

1945047

1 Lynn stepped out onto the patio and stopped short. When she saw them coming, she turned to go back in, but she tripped over Timothy's skateboard.

"Lynn," her oldest brother Matthew called. "Wait. I want you to meet Sarah." Timothy was with them, showing off for Matthew's new girl friend, Miss Sarah Lawrence.

Lynn knew in advance that no girl was good enough for Matthew. She watched them, the girl looking tiny between the two boys, both of them over six feet. At barely fourteen Lynn herself was five nine and very self-conscious about it.

"Sarah, this is my kid sister Lynn," Matthew was saying. He had his arm around the shoulders of this paragon of women. Lynn noticed at once that Miss Sarah Lawrence had perfect teeth. She herself still wore her retainers, and although a counselor at that awful camp her mother had sent her to last summer to achieve poise had told her, "If you feel tongue-tied, honey, and can't think of anything to say, just smile," Lynn avoided too much smiling.

"I'm awfully glad to meet you," Miss Sarah Lawrence was saying. "I've heard so much about you."

"The kid monster," Timothy said. Timothy was sixteen, and at the present stage of his life, his greatest joy came from putting down his sister.

Lynn muttered something that came out a mixture of "hi" and "how do you do" because in the middle of it she remembered her mother scolding her for saying "hi" when she was introduced. She blushed and started to turn away.

"Lynnie is our ace conversationalist," Timothy said. "She talks up a storm night and day."

Lynn shot a fierce look at him.

"Knock it off, Tim," Matthew said, but he was too engrossed in Miss Sarah Lawrence to make the strong defense of his sister that he usually did. "Sis, do you know where Mom is?"

"Library," Lynn said and escaped into the house. It was going to be nice to have Matthew home, as soon as they got rid of Miss Sarah Lawrence. Although she couldn't absolutely relax until she was sure she had persuaded her mother not to send her back to the awful camp. It ought to be clear that it had been a total waste of money.

She went up to her room, where she was relatively

safe, and lay down on her bed. She thought over all the gracious things she ought to have said to Miss Sarah Lawrence. She stretched her arms back over her head and groaned. With all her might she longed for the days before she was twelve. The golden days when she wasn't tall, didn't have any hardware in her mouth, didn't have to think and rethink everything she wanted to say until she found the moment for saying it was gone, didn't feel that everyone's critical eyes were on her, and wasn't harried and driven by a thousand emotions that she couldn't even name.

She had always been quiet and shy, but there hadn't been this agony of self-consciousness and cold, gripping fear that made her abrupt and silent when she longed to be friendly. She knew she was her mother's despair. Her mother was gregarious, witty, self-possessed, sure of herself. She couldn't understand at all this child she had produced. Lynn's father was more like his daughter, but although he gave her sympathetic glances and sometimes mildly rebuked Timothy, his own inarticulateness made him not much of an ally. Matthew understood her and defended her, but he'd been away at college for three years. Her other brother Sam was always busy—first Scouts and camp and a hundred school activities, now college and this summer the Army Reserve.

She heard her mother calling her after a while. She went downstairs to help get the dinner on. Her mother was bubbling with enthusiasm about Miss Sarah Lawrence.

"Isn't she a doll? She's the best one Matt's brought home yet. Do stand up straight, Lynnie. You look like a wilted string bean when you slump like that. Put the sweet potatoes in the Paul Revere bowl, will you? And remind your father to wash up. We're almost ready. I hope you'll make friends with Sarah. Do try to talk to her."

"I will," Lynn mumbled.

"Did Matt tell you he's going to summer school?"

"No." Lynn's heart sank. He'd be gone again, then. "You aren't going to send me to that camp, are you, Mother?"

Her mother turned and looked at her thoughtfully, the stirring spoon held suspended over the sauce for the ham. "I don't know. I don't really think it did much."

"It didn't do a thing. It made me worse."

"Well, we'll see. Get the potatoes onto the hot tray. Please straighten up, Lynn. Don't you see how nicely Sarah carries herself? And please, for my sake, do talk a little at dinner. She'll think you don't like her."

"Or that I'm retarded," Lynn said bitterly. She went to warn her father about dinner, and she thought of the great plan one of the counselors had had last summer "to bring Lynn out of her shell." She had been forced to come to dinner each night with an anecdote to tell the others at the table. Lynn had done it, but it had been one of the most humiliating experiences of her life.

Her father was in his study reading student papers. He taught geography at the college. He looked at her over his glasses. "I always thought," he said, "that Sarah Lawrence was a college." He got up and stretched. "Well, she's a pretty child."

"Dinner in five minutes," Lynn said.

At dinner she sat between Matthew and her father, opposite Miss Sarah Lawrence. Everybody seemed to be in a gay mood, even her father. She listened to the conversation, tried to smile, thought of a couple of brilliant remarks and discarded them.

"Lynn," her mother said in her disapproving voice, "can't you pass the rolls to Sarah?"

Lynn jumped and dropped her own roll, which fell to the floor. Matthew retrieved it quickly and quietly, but Timothy sang out "Butter Fingers" to the opening notes of "Goldfinger."

"That's enough, Timothy," his father said, more sharply than usual.

But Timothy was hard to suppress. "Matthew is the learned one," he said to Sarah, "Sam is the popular one, I'm the athletic one, and Lynn is the shy one." He grinned because he knew the family had expected him to say something worse. "Lynn is so shy, she hangs a blanket over her full-length mirror."

"That's like Amy Lowell," Miss Sarah Lawrence said.

"I don't know Amy."

She laughed. "She was a poet in the early part of the century. She was very heavy, and she hated to look in mirrors, so she always draped them in black."

"Well, Lynnie's not heavy," Matthew said.

"No, of course not. I was just thinking of the mirror thing . . ." Miss Sarah Lawrence saw that she had been tactless, and she was momentarily embarrassed.

But Lynn was thinking of Amy Lowell. That was one of the saddest things she'd ever heard. It was only the bottom part of her own mirror that she sometimes draped, because she hated how long her legs were. It was mean of Timothy to have told.

During the dessert the telephone rang. Timothy got it and called his father. "It's for you, Dad."

When her father came back to the table, Lynn looked up at him and saw that something had happened. His face looked shiny with happiness. Whatever it was, she was glad.

"What is it?" his wife asked.

He struck a pose. "Ladies and gentlemen, you are looking at the Fulbright lecturer in geography for the Free University of Brussels, Belgium, Europe."

There was a moment of surprised silence, and then his wife jumped up and hugged him. "You got it!"

"I thought you were only an alternate," Matthew said.

"I was. Mason can't go."

There was an explosion of excitement from the others, but Lynn sat quite still.

Her mother threw her an impatient look. "Well, Lynn. Congratulate your dad."

"Does that mean," Lynn said slowly, "that we have to go to Belgium?"

"*Have* to!" Miss Sarah Lawrence sounded disbelieving.

"Europe, Lynn," Matthew said. "You'll love it."

Lynn pushed back her chair. "I'll hate it." She saw her father's hurt look. "I'm glad you got it, but I can't . . . I can't . . ." She stopped because she knew she would burst into tears in a minute.

"Of all the stupid things," Timothy said, glaring at her.

"I can't . . . I can't even speak French," she said, struggling to explain her horror at the idea.

"You can't even speak English," Timothy said.

"Shut up, Tim," Matthew said.

And her mother said coldly, "Lynn, I think you had better go to your room. This is too fine a moment for your father, to be spoiled by your selfishness."

2 She was grounded for a week, although her mother always said that was just the opposite of what ought to be done. So she was also given a long lecture on selfishness by her mother. She went to her father and apologized.

He looked at her thoughtfully. "I know you didn't mean it the way it sounded to your mother. You're scared, aren't you."

She nodded. Tears stung her eyes. Lately she was ready to cry at everything. It made her furious with herself.

"Your mother can't understand it because she loves new people and new situations. But you're more like me, I guess, poor kid." He paused and knocked the tobacco out of his pipe. "It's worst of all at your age, but to this day when I face a roomful of new students at the start of a semester, my impulse is to run."

She stood in front of him in silence, not knowing what to say. She wanted to tell him she appreciated his being so nice about it.

"Well, let me think about it. Maybe I can think of something."

But she didn't see what he could think of. It was a hopeless situation. She talked for a long time to her best friend Mary Alice, telling her the whole story. Mary

Alice, of course, would have loved to go to Belgium, but although she didn't understand Lynn's shyness, she accepted her as she was and gave her sympathy and loyalty.

Matthew was gone, driving Miss Sarah Lawrence home and then going up to register for summer school. He would be back for a few days. Sam breezed in on a twenty-four-hour pass, shared in the excitement over the news, wished he could go with them, assured Lynn she would love it, and gave her his book of conversational French.

Matthew came back the day after her period of being grounded had ended. When she had finished stacking the dishes into the dishwasher, which her mother usually didn't let her do because she was afraid Lynn would break something, she was summoned to her father's study, where she found her parents and Matthew.

Her father opened the conversation. "We've been trying to think what to do about you, honey," he said. "How to solve your dilemma."

"Your very *peculiar* dilemma," her mother said.

"Let me talk, Ella," he said.

Lynn looked at him with dread. It was unusual, in itself, for him to take command in a family discussion.

"I know how you feel. When I was a kid, I got yanked around from pillar to post, one school after another. It was one of the bad things about being an Army brat."

"But Europe is hardly—" her mother began.

"Ella, please. We've talked about it a good deal, pro and con," he said.

Lynn wanted to ask "pro and con what?" but she remained silent.

"Matthew had an idea that we thought you might like."

"What is it?" She looked at Matthew. Could she still trust him or had he gone over to the Miss Sarah Lawrences and the other grown-ups?

"Would you like to spend the year with Grandmother?" Matthew said.

"With Grandmother!" It was so unexpected, she couldn't quite get it through her head. She had never thought of it.

"You've always been close to your grandmother," her father said, "and you love Nantucket."

It was true. Next to Matthew she loved her grandmother more than anybody in the world. They were close friends, sometimes almost co-conspirators. Because of that awful camp, she hadn't gone on the annual summer visit to Grandmother last year, and she had missed her. It was two years now since she had seen her.

"Why don't you say something?" her mother burst out.

"Take it easy, Mom," Matthew said.

"Well, she's so . . . so slow about everything. You never know what she's thinking."

"I'd love to go to Grandmother's," Lynn said in a

loud, clear voice. No Belgians, no strange language and customs to cope with, no teasing Timothy, no critical mother. "She won't be ashamed of me the way you are."

Her mother looked shocked. "Ashamed! What a thing to say. Ashamed of my own child!"

Lynn wanted to say, "You see? That's why I don't say anything. When I do say something, it's the wrong thing." But she only said, "I mean I embarrass you."

Before her mother could explode again, Lynn's father said, "Then we'll call Doris tonight and see what she thinks. Personally I'll be just as glad to have someone with her. She's not getting any younger."

"Mother?" his wife said. "She'll never grow old."

"Well, those people told you she was getting forgetful."

"What do they know. They're not even Islanders."

Matthew and his father laughed. They were always amused by her conviction that if a person hadn't been born and reared on Nantucket, as she had been, there was something not quite right about him, no matter how acceptable he might be in every other way.

"You can laugh," she said, "but Islanders know each other. And Mother was just fine last summer, as far as I could see. She'll always be all right. She's the strongest woman on the island."

"And man, that's some strong," Matthew said, accenting the "some," the way Nantucketers did when they wanted to be emphatic.

"So are you happy now?" Lynn's father said to her.

"Yes," she said. She gave her father a quick hug, "I won't be a worry to you."

"You aren't a worry," he said. "You're my daughter, and I want you to be happy." It was a lot for him to say.

"You're going to have to be helpful to your grandmother," her mother said. "Help with the housework. Be careful not to break things. Your grandmother loves her things."

"Oh, don't lecture her now, Mom," Matthew said. "Let's call Grandmother."

And so it was settled. During the weeks before it was time to go, Lynn was left pretty much alone, as her mother packed and unpacked and packed again, found a tenant for the house, dealt with banks and insurance and all the rest of the details that she enjoyed. Lynn spent most of her time with Mary Alice, and tried to keep hidden somewhere at the back of her mind the fact that even at Grandmother's, she would have to deal with a new school.

3 Lynn leaned on the railing of the steamer *Nantucket* watching her brother Matthew getting smaller and smaller on the wharf at Wood's Hole, as the ship eased out of the harbor. She had mixed feelings—

excitement about going to Nantucket after so long a time away, eagerness to see her grandmother, an unexpected feeling of loss at her family's departure for Europe that morning, and a much stronger sense of loss as Matthew blurred in the distance. There was also the anxiety about school that gnawed at her mind, which she tried hard not to think about. She had to go to school somewhere after all, and even her own school hadn't been any bed of roses for the last couple of years. Yet a new school . . .

She felt a little seasick, though the water was calm. She swallowed one of Matthew's Dramamine tablets.

Her parents and Timothy had been excited as they went off to board their plane. Why couldn't she be excited about a change, too. Sam had made arrangements to take a year at the university in Brussels, so he would be joining them later in the month. Only she and Matthew were to be left on this side of the ocean. It gave her a funny feeling.

Well, she couldn't hang on the rail and mope all the way to Nantucket. She found a chair on the forward deck and settled down for the three-hour trip. There were quite a few people on board for the middle of the week. Probably most of them would get off at Martha's Vineyard. Some of the young ones with backpacks were obviously day-trippers.

A man, about thirty-five years old, who was sitting near her, opened one eye and looked at her. He nodded, and she was afraid he was going to talk to her, but he closed his eyes again. He looked vaguely familiar. Maybe he was an Islander, although he didn't look like one.

She tried to relax. Herring gulls looking for garbage hovered over the ship. They would stay all the way to the Island. A little girl was tossing crumbs at them, and they swooped to catch them with expert timing and grace. Lynn watched them through half-closed eyes. Behind them the sky looked almost lavender.

She went to sleep and woke up later as the boat eased into the wharf at Martha's Vineyard. The crew threw out the lines and docked the boat with the careless competence of long practice. The disembarking passengers gathered near the gangplank and in a few minutes began to shuffle off, back to the familiar element of earth. But an island, Lynn thought, is really only an illusion of earth. It came up out of the sea, and it could fall right in again. It was an unsettling thought for a person who was going to spend a year on an island a lot farther out to sea than this one.

Sometimes it seemed to her as if the whole earth rocked under her, and she got dizzy thinking about its spinning on its axis. Her father said people got disturbing thoughts like that in their adolescence. She had so many more years of adolescence to live through. Sometimes she wondered how she would ever make it.

The boat rocked in the swell and she took a candy bar

out of her pocket to distract herself. The man near her woke up and said, "Where are we? East Chop?"

His voice startled Lynn. Her mind had been so far away. She hoped he wasn't going to start a conversation. It made her very nervous when people she didn't know spoke to her.

He looked at the wharf as the boat began to pull away again. "No, it's Vineyard Haven. Got rid of the day-trippers, did we?"

Lynn smiled stiffly, remembered her retainers, and put out the smile. He got up and stood at the rail, looking down at the roiled water. His curly hair was just turning gray, and he looked scrubbed and clean, although he wore a pair of faded jeans and a blue sweater with leather-patched elbows.

After a minute he disappeared.

"Here you go." He was back, holding out a hot dog. In his other hand, he had one for himself.

She wanted to refuse it, but that would be rude. Not that she wasn't hungry, but the hot dog might be an attempt to buy conversation from her. She took it and muttered her "thank you." He sat down and ate his.

"Not exactly Lucullan fare, but if you're hungry enough . . ." He shaded his eyes with his hand. "It feels as if we're on a long voyage to faraway places, doesn't it. I think that every time I come. Where will we end up? Fiji? Samoa? Pago Pago? The New Hebrides?" He had been talking without looking at her, but he turned in his chair now and smiled at her.

She had to say something.

"Wrong ocean," she said.

He laughed. "Right you are."

He settled himself deep in the canvas chair. "Call me if we run into any hurricanes." And he went to sleep.

She woke in half an hour or so and went inside for a Coke. The man was still asleep. He must not get enough sleep at home, she thought. She wondered what he did.

There were not many people on the boat now. She walked around the deck a few times, taking deep breaths of good salty air. As they got nearer to Nantucket, she leaned on the rail watching for the first landfall.

Somebody said, "There it is!" And she made out the black cylinder of the water tank that was halfway between Madaket and the jetties. Her heart began to pound. Oh, she hoped Grandmother would still like her. It had been two years, and she had done all that growing. But Grandmother wouldn't care.

Gulls swooped and dove over the bow of the ship. The yellow beaches came into sight, and the sun turned the shingled roofs silver and danced off the gilded dome of the Old South Church. Lynn imagined that she could already smell the bayberry bushes in the meadows. She thought of Grandmother's house, once a small cottage when she had married Grandfather and come to live on the island, but now a rambling vine-covered house that had grown to accommodate the growing family. Grandmother was from California and had gone to Pomona College. It was going to be strange to be in Nantucket all winter. She had never been there after Labor Day.

The boat's whistle hooted as they inched through the channel to Steamboat Wharf, past dozens of sailboats. Lynn got her suitcase and the little case of miniatures that she always kept with her. Once there had been a dollhouse for them, but her mother had decided when Lynn was eleven that she was too old for it and had given it to the Good Will. Matthew had given her a tiny glass horse this morning.

The boat scraped along the wharf. The lower gangplank, where the cars were, went down, and then the passenger gangplank. She hurried off the boat looking for Grandmother. Taxis were lined up for customers, and there were cars and station wagons belonging to people meeting friends and relatives, but no old blue Buick, no Grandmother. Dismayed, Lynn looked at her watch. Was the boat early? No, it was actually four minutes late. Grandmother hadn't come!

4 She walked up the pier looking for her grandmother. She felt panicky. Grandmother never forgot things. If she wasn't there, maybe it meant she didn't
want Lynn to come? But Lynn knew that made no
sense. When her parents had called, Grandmother had
said for her to come. Maybe she had had a terrible accident. Or become ill. Old people had things happen to
them.

She stubbed her toe on a plank and dropped her suitcase. Thank goodness she hadn't dropped the case full of
miniatures. The man in the blue sweater said, "Oops.
Here, I'll get it." He picked it up and smiled at her.

"Thank you." She reached for it, but he didn't give it
to her right away.

"Is somebody meeting you?"

"Yes."

He turned as an attractive woman in jeans ran down
the pier toward him. He did then put down the suitcase
and his own plaid canvas bag, to embrace the woman.
They looked at each other in obvious delight. "Hi!" he
said to her. "Miss me?"

"Not for a minute." She laughed and kissed him again.
"Come on."

"Wait a second." He turned to Lynn again. "Can we

drop you off somewhere? My name is Ault. This is my wife."

Lynn felt confused. Things weren't going right. "No," she said. "I mean, I'm glad to meet you. But I'll be all right. My grandmother will be here . . ."

"Who is your grandmother, dear?" Mrs. Ault said.

"Mrs. Linley. In Madaket."

"Oh, sure. We know Mrs. Linley." She and her husband exchanged glances. "Look, she may have forgotten. Let us drop you off. We live near Trotts Hills, on Eel Point Road."

Lynn stood still for a moment, and then she realized she had to say something. "I couldn't bother you. Anyway she might come and miss me."

"I'll call her up," Mrs. Ault said. "Gerald, put Miss Linley's things in the car. I'll call from the phone on Straight Wharf."

"I'm not Miss Linley," Lynn said. "I'm Lynn Grenville. My grandmother is my mother's mother . . ."

"Oh, I've met your dad," the man said. He was already carrying Lynn's things, and there was nothing she could do but follow him. "I came across him one time when he was clamming in his secret spot. He had to let me in on the secret because I was there. We wallowed around in the mud for an hour, getting little necks."

"He's gone to Europe," Lynn said. "He got a Fulbright."

"Wonderful." He let down the tailgate of a Ford station wagon and put his own bag and her things in the back. "I liked him very much. Are you going to stay with Mrs. Linley all winter?"

"Yes." She still felt panicky. Where could Grandmother be? "I don't know where my grandmother can be," she said.

He opened the door for her. "She may have forgotten. We all get forgetful when the years creep up on us."

"Oh, I don't think so. She's never been like that."

"Seen her lately?"

"No, not for two years."

He nodded. "You may find that she's gotten a little older. She'll find that you have too, I expect."

Mrs. Ault came back in a few minutes. "She thought it was tomorrow. She's so sorry." Getting in beside Lynn, she added, "Well, I'm glad we were here. It's a long hike to Madaket with luggage."

Lynn tried to get rid of the feeling of dread. She knew it was only because things hadn't gone according to plan. Really, there was nothing to dread. These nice people would take her to the cottage. But it was strange that Grandmother had gotten mixed-up. She had always been so efficient. She even used to remember from summer to summer what each of her grandchildren liked to eat. With Lynn it was always seafood, especially clams.

Because she felt she ought to say something, she asked whether they lived here year round.

"No," Mrs. Ault said. "My husband is a doctor. We live in Boston, but we spend as much time here as we can."

"Which is never enough," he said.

As the doctor drove slowly along the narrow, cobbled street, Lynn forgot everything except her pleasure in being on the island again. Nothing had changed that she could see. The Pacific National Bank was still there and the Atheneum Library and the Maria Mitchell Library. There were the old houses with their widow walks, built close to the sidewalk and "cheek by jowl," as her father said. There were the green benches where Main and Center streets came together.

Then the doctor cut off onto the Madaket Road, and they were out of town, driving through moorland with ground cover cropped close by the winds. Past the Ram Pasture, past the Sheep Pond, the treeless view exposing the dunes and the sea. They passed bicyclists leaning into the light wind.

"There's a fish crow," Dr. Ault said, pointing to a bird on a fence post.

Lynn smelled the sharp smell of the salt sea.

"It rained early this morning," Mrs. Ault said.

"Rain before seven, clear before eleven." Dr. Ault slowed down as they came to Madaket.

Her heart was beating fast. It was wonderful to be here. It was like finding some part of herself that she had mislaid.

"I'm glad you're here," Dr. Ault said. "It must get pretty lonely for your grandmother."

He carried her things up the little hedge-lined walk to the front door, and there stood Grandmother, framed in rambler rose vines, holding out her arms.

"Lynn!"

"Grandmother . . ." She remembered to thank Dr. Ault and to wave to Mrs. Ault before they drove off, and then she let her grandmother lead her into the sitting room.

Grandmother's eyes were shining. "Let me look at you. You've grown some big. I don't know as I'd have known you."

Lynn grinned. She felt reassured now that she was here. Grandmother didn't look a bit older, unless maybe a few little wrinkles around her eyes that hadn't been there before. Her cheeks were still pink and soft, her eyes were just as blue as before and as full of interest and delight. She still stood straight and tall. "You look wonderful. Mother and everybody send their love."

"You must tell me all the news. Wait, let me take your things up to your room."

"Oh, I can take them."

"I'm giving you your mother's room at the head of the stairs. I'll make some hot chocolate, you used to like that. Oh, Lynn, I can't think how I got the days mixed-up."

"Oh, I get days mixed-up all the time." Lynn ran upstairs with her things. She felt as if some contented bee were humming inside her.

She looked around. She had never stayed in this room. It was the biggest of the upstairs bedrooms. Grandmother's chintz curtains hung at the casement windows, and there was the pitched roof that made you stoop when you went near the walls. She sat for a moment in her favorite chair, the Boston rocker with the stencilled gold eagle. The old china pitcher and basin still stood on the commode, although Grandmother had had inside plumbing for years and years.

She unpacked her miniatures and arranged them on the bureau: the glass animals together, the tiny maple highboy with the brass pulls on the drawers that worked, the Governor Winthrop desk three inches tall, with the tiny eraser and the miniature newspaper inside it that said *Chicago Tribune* and which you had to read with a magnifying glass, except for the headline. She put out her tiny crystal chandelier and the hurricane lamp, the sofa with the purple velvet cushion, the two-inch cradle. She picked up the beautifully wrought rooster and said to him, "Okay, now, you guys. You're in Nantucket, and that's going to be home. Got that?" She set him down carefully.

Her mother said it was grotesque for a girl who was already five feet nine to be playing with miniatures. But her father and Matthew went on giving her things for her collection, so they must not think she was nuts. Last Christmas Matthew had given her a charm bracelet, and she had brought that with her, too. It had an elephant, a horse, a cat, and a fish, so far.

Lynn checked the bookcase in the hall, to see if *Cranford* was there. She had been reading *Cranford* off and on ever since she could remember, whenever she came to Grandmother's.

By the time she got downstairs, Grandmother had put one of her hand-embroidered luncheon cloths on the gateleg table, and there were thin bread and butter and cucumber sandwiches as well as the flowered pot full of steaming hot chocolate.

"Sit down and pitch in," her grandmother said. She brought in a little cut glass pitcher of cream to top off the cocoa.

Lynn ate a sandwich dreamily and sighed. "Grandmother, everything you have is the prettiest I ever saw."

Her grandmother smiled. "I'm glad. I'm afraid things are going a bit to rack and ruin around here. I don't have the energy I used to have." She frowned again, as if this puzzled and worried her. "I don't know what's the matter with me." She played absently with a teaspoon.

"Well, now I can help."

Her grandmother brightened. "Oh, it will be so nice to have you here. Now tell me all about everything. Where is it they're going? Somewhere in Europe. Was it Holland?"

"No, Belgium." Lynn ate her sandwiches and drank the delicious cocoa as she told Grandmother all the news.

"Isn't that nice," Grandmother said when she had finished. "I'm some relieved your mother married that nice, ambitious boy."

It took Lynn a second to realize that she was talking about her father. She had never thought of him as a nice, ambitious boy.

"She was engaged to that Macy boy, you know, the one that didn't amount to anything. Most Macys amount to a whole lot, but that one was the bad egg in the basket."

Lynn grinned. The old stories of her parents' youth had been told and retold until they were shiny with telling. She knew all about the Macy boy. According to her mother's version, he was a handsome, blond, Viking type; but her father, who had never met him, said he was no-good; and Lynn's mother would laugh and say, "What do you know? You're an off-islander."

"At first your grandfather didn't take to your father. It's hard for a Nantucket man to accept the idea of his favorite daughter marrying an off-islander. Although he married me." She chuckled. She folded her old, strong hands around the warmth of the teacup, and her gaze was far away. After a moment she straightened up. "No use getting broody. You want more cocoa? Help yourself, child."

But although she wanted more, Lynn hesitated to lift

the pretty china chocolate pot. She dropped things so often. She hoped and prayed she wouldn't break any of Grandmother's pretty things.

Grandmother sat looking into her teacup, lost again in thought. Not knowing quite what to do, Lynn sat still. It wasn't like Grandmother to be so abstracted. Maybe that doctor was right, and she had been alone too much. Lynn didn't know whether to get up or sit there.

Minutes went by. She coughed politely.

Her grandmother started and looked up. "Sakes, Ella!" she said. "Time to put the chicken in the oven." She got up briskly and went to the kitchen.

Lynn listened to the sound of pans rattling, oven door opening. She felt a little scared. Grandmother had called her by her mother's name. Didn't she know she was Lynn?

5 She held her hands out to make sure they were steady, and then she carefully carried the chocolate pot to the kitchen, putting it on the big old scarred kitchen table with a sigh of relief. She got her cup and Grandmother's teacup and brought them too. Nothing dropped, nothing spilled.

"What can I do to help?"

"Nothing, darling. Why don't you get a bit of rest? We'll have supper at six. I'm an old country woman, you know. I eat early."

"Oh, I like to eat early. I'm always hungry."

Her grandmother laughed, wiped her hands on her apron and hugged Lynn. "Of course you are. You've grown so tall, Lynn."

Lynn felt a wave of relief. She did know she was Lynn. Calling her Ella must have been a slip of the tongue. Her own mother sometimes mixed up the children's names, even called Lynn, "Tim" or "Sam," and then they'd all laugh. For a moment she thought of them flying over the ocean and she missed them fiercely. There had been a little time just at first this afternoon when she'd felt strange with Grandmother, with the tight sick feeling in her stomach that she got with strangers, but that was all gone now, and Grandmother was somebody she could talk to, like Matthew or Mary Alice.

"I'm hooking a rug for your mother," Grandmother said. "I'll show it to you after supper. Why don't you run along now and get some rest before we eat. Chicken tonight, with gravy."

Lynn ran up the narrow old stairs, almost forgetting to duck at the top where the ceiling was low. Things were going to be all right. Kids on Nantucket wouldn't seem anywhere near as strange and frightening as kids in Belgium would have. At least they'd speak English.

She took a shower and lay down with *Cranford*, but she fell asleep. It was almost dark when she awoke. She could hear Grandmother rattling pots and pans and singing "O Jerusalem, Happy Land." She combed her hair and went downstairs. The chicken smelled wonderful.

But in the door of the dining room she stopped and stared. The table was beautifully set, as Grandmother always set it, with her sterling and her lace tablecloth and her Irish linen napkins. A slender crystal vase with two roses stood in the middle. But there was only one place at the table. Lynn felt as if somebody had hit her in the stomach. She leaned against the wainscoting.

Then her grandmother's voice with surprise in it, said, "Lynn! Lynn, dear. You're going to have supper with me. Of course, you are. Isn't it lovely?" She lifted her hand to her head. "Did I forget?"

She looked frightened. Forgetting her own fear, Lynn went to her and put her arms around her. "You bet I'm going to have supper with you. I'm here to stay, Grandma, and I'm so happy."

Her grandmother's frown didn't go away. "How could I have forgotten? You came on the boat, didn't you. Today?"

"This afternoon. I'm going to stay, remember? Mama and the rest of them have gone to Europe."

"How nice," her grandmother said. She sat down heavily. "Lynn, I'm getting old. I forget things."

"Oh, it doesn't matter, Grandmother. I'm only fourteen, and I forget things, too." But it did matter. She had counted on Grandmother's solid presence, on her strong sense of herself, to lean against in her own insecurity. But it wasn't there. Grandmother forgot. She forgot Lynn was there. How could she?

Lynn went into the kitchen because she was afraid she was going to burst into tears. She didn't know what to do. She wanted to call up Matthew, but what could Matthew do? He couldn't take her to college with him. What was she to do?

In a few minutes Grandmother came into the kitchen, and she seemed like herself again. "Will you put the cranberry bowl on the table, Lynnie? I'll just finish this gravy. And the potatoes are ready. Will you have milk?"

"Thank you." Struggling to keep herself steady, Lynn carried the cranberry bowl to the table. She was going to have to tell Grandmother that she dropped things a lot. But Grandmother wouldn't remember it.

"Is something the matter?" Grandmother had brought in the platter of chicken.

"I'd better tell you," Lynn said. "I drop things a lot lately. I'd hate to break any of your pretty dishes."

Her grandmother looked at her closely. "Now if you were Ella, I'd say you were making that up to get out of helping, but you're an honest child. Why do you drop things? Are you nervous?"

"Yes, I guess I'm nervous." Lynn had never known her mother made up stories to get out of work. That was interesting.

"Well, I get nervous, too. We'll try to help each other not to get nervous."

"I can't imagine you nervous."

"Can't you?" Grandmother smiled. "When you are responsible for a large family, you learn to hide your nervousness. But it builds up, like a volcano, I suppose, and some day when you aren't responsible any more, you begin to get little eruptions." She arranged the chicken platter and sighed. "Let us hope there won't be a big one."

"Mother says it's adolescence with me."

"Yes, well, perhaps. I've always thought that words like 'adolescence' and 'senior citizen' were convenient pegs to hang a person on when he got a little bothersome one way or another. But there, what do I know. In my day we didn't have much psychology."

"I don't believe in psychology," Lynn said.

Grandmother went to the kitchen to get the gravy, and Lynn thought she would have forgotten the topic of conversation by the time she got back. But she hadn't.

She said, "I won't go that far. I believe Freud shed a lot of light. But like everything else, it can turn glib and superficial." She set the gravy bowl on the table. "You bring your glass of milk, dear. And don't worry.

If it falls, it falls. My dishes will all go to you in time anyway, since you're the only girl in the family, so you'd just be breaking your own things. You don't have to feel guilty."

Lynn brought the milk and set it down.

Her grandmother held the carving knife poised over the chicken. "I seem to remember you like white meat. Am I right?"

"Yes, please." It was astonishing the little things Grandmother did remember.

"Help yourself to squash. It's out of my garden."

"This is wonderful chicken," Lynn said. "And you make the best gravy in the world."

Grandmother chuckled. "You're a flatterer."

"No, not really. Sometimes I think of really nice things I'd like to say to people, but by the time I'm ready to say them, the conversation is about something else."

"Your grandfather never could flatter people. He made enemies saying what he thought. I used to tell him, 'Aaron, if you'd just think before you speak. A little diplomacy never hurt.' But he never did. He made some mortal enemies. But by and large he was well liked. Got elected Shellfish Warden eleven years running."

Through dinner Lynn's mind ran on two tracks. One part listened to Grandmother's reminiscences about Grandfather and their early life on the island, which she loved to hear, the other half trying to think what she could do to make school on the island go right. What if she tried diplomacy? Maybe she wouldn't feel so big and so out of place, if she could just make people like her so much they wouldn't notice her size. She was willing to try anything.

Grandmother went to bed very soon after the dishes were done. "I'm sorry if I seem rude, dear, but I do get tired."

In a way Lynn was glad to escape to her own room. It had been a long, changing day, and she had a lot to think about. First of all, how to become a diplomatic person. She lay down on her comfortable bed, listening to the wind, trying to think how to be somebody who made other people feel good.

6 Lynn was up early the next morning, but her grandmother was ahead of her. Within a few minutes she was eating blueberry pancakes.

"The low bush berries are nearly gone," her grandmother said. "We had a good crop this year. What are you going to do today?"

Lynn was looking out the window at the glossy green leaves of the japonica. "Just mess around."

Grandmother laughed. She had a nice laugh, low and quiet and amused. "That sounds nice." She passed Lynn the platter of scrambled eggs. "They say they're full of cholesterol, but to my way of thinking, you can't do better than an egg. Well, the summer is nearly over. Enjoy the outdoors while you can. I hope we'll have a long fall."

1945047

Over the dishes later she said, "We'll have to do something about your school, I guess. Dear me. It's a long time since I've enrolled a child in school. Do you still send them off with a book bag and a sandwich? No, it's bound to be more complicated nowadays. Computers and all that."

"Don't worry about it. I'll take care of it." A dazzling idea had shot through Lynn's mind, on the heels of the dismay she had felt at hearing the word school.

"All right, dear. If they want me to sign anything, bring it home."

Lynn set off toward the beach, the idea still dancing in her mind. It was completely crazy. She could never get away with it. If Grandmother were always forgetful, it might work, but she wasn't. She tried to stop thinking about her idea, but it was so attractive, she couldn't get it out of her head.

Grandmother had said she was an honest child. She preferred to be honest. For one thing, it was easier. The idea she was thinking of would take an awful lot of hard planning and deception, and she was bound to slip up sooner or later. But could she . . . was there a chance . . . could she possibly get away with not going to school at all?

Of course not. It was insane. She angled off in a northeasterly direction toward the beach, past the houses, past Fishers Landing. She saw the Eel Point Road sign and thought briefly of the Aults. Like the other summer people, they would be gone after Labor Day.

Some of the cottages were already closed, their shuttered faces toward the sea. After Labor Day the island settled down to being itself, putting up its storm windows, getting in firewood and coal. Books that hadn't been picked up all summer would be companions again, and the TV sets would be on. There'd be fewer people to notice what you did. On the other hand, the ones left might notice you more.

Her mother had said Grandmother didn't see people enough, had even stopped going to church because it hurt her knees to kneel.

"Your mother was always a solitary person," Lynn's father had said to her. "She's just a little more so since your father died."

That could be a real advantage if Lynn tried to avoid school. But sooner or later Grandmother would notice, or someone would mention it to her. It was very chancy. What would happen to her, though, if she tried it and Grandmother found out? A scolding, maybe, but Grandmother never scolded hard. It couldn't be as bad as going to a new school. There was no way it could.

Lynn ran down the hard sand, forgetting her problem for a minute in the joy of being here. There was a stiff wind, but the sun was bright and the blue water danced with light.

She threw herself down behind a dune to get her breath. A little cloud of sandhoppers rose up from a pile of seaweed, and a hermit crab scuttled away. Over her head gulls wheeled, and inland a short distance a harrier flew low, crying out his *chu-chu-chu*. Sandpipers ran down the beach as if they had met with some domestic disaster.

Lynn stretched out on her stomach, her chin propped on her hands, and wished she could stay here forever. She loved watching all the strange things to be found at the beach. Maybe she'd be a beachcomber when she grew up.

Three girls came racing along the beach, headed toward her. Lynn moved back further into the protection of the dune, hoping they wouldn't see her.

She thought they were going by, but suddenly the one in the lead swerved. She was almost upon Lynn when she saw her. She stopped short with a yelp of surprise. The other two, one about the same age and a smaller one, caught up with her. They stared at Lynn.

The first one said, "Who are you?"

Lynn hesitated.

The little one said, "She's summer people."

"What's your name?"

"Lynn Grenville."

"Never heard of her," the second girl said.

The little one said, "Are you a grown-up or a child?"

"She's too long to be a child," the second one said.

"She looks like a child in the face," the first one said.

Lynn hated being discussed as if she weren't there. "What's your name?" she said, to interrupt them.

"I'm Susan Coffin. That's my sister Patty." She pointed to the little one.

"I'm Biddy Sondheim," the other girl said. They looked rather alike, all blonde and tanned and sturdy.

"Where do you go to school?" Biddy asked.

Lynn gave the name of her school at home. "It's near Boston." She wished they would go away.

"We're going to have a new homeroom teacher," Biddy said. "And is she ever going to wish she'd never been born."

"She's from Boston," Susan said, staring at Lynn with clear hostility, as if it were Lynn's fault.

"Why will she be sorry?" Lynn didn't want to prolong the conversation, but she was curious.

"They're layin' plans," Patty said, ducking her head toward the older girls.

"Hush!" Susan said fiercely.

"What kind of plans?" Lynn asked.

"Secret plans." Susan kicked at Patty. "Don't tell."

"I will too," Patty said. "They're going to get a lot of pop bottles and . . ." She ducked as Susan aimed her foot at her again.

Lynn couldn't help asking. They sounded so ominous. "Pop bottles for what? Are you going to throw them at the teacher?"

" 'Course not," Biddy said. "That might kill her and then we'd get the chair."

Susan looked up and down the empty beach and spoke in a low voice. "What we do is, we have them in our desks, every kid has to have at least three. When the captain gives the signal . . ."

"Susan is the captain," Patty said.

"I give the signal and we roll our bottles down the aisles, hard, right at her. We've been practicing. It makes a terrible noise. Some will probably smash."

Lynn was impressed. "Are you really going to?"

"It's wicked," Patty said.

"Off-islander teachers are wicked," Susan said, sticking out her jaw. "They got it coming."

"Any kid that won't do it, we drum him out of the regiment," Biddy said.

Patty said, "And that *hurts*."

"It don't kill them," Susan said.

"Won't you get expelled?" Lynn asked.

"They can't expel a whole class. Anyway kids do things like that. Kids are tough on this island."

"Last year," Biddy said, "the tenth grade boys hung

the science teacher out the window by his heels. Just let him hang there awhile."

Susan fixed Lynn with glittering eyes. "He was from Boston, too."

"He resigned the next day," Biddy said.

"It was that night," Susan said. "We don't want off-islanders here." She turned and ran off up the beach, and the other two followed.

Lynn felt sick. An ordinary school was bad enough, but how could she survive in a tough school like that? Already they hated her, just because she was an off-islander. She'd be drummed out of the regiment first thing. And she didn't doubt that it hurt.

She watched them disappear way down the beach. In her school at home there were tough kids. Some were mean, some smoked pot and got into trouble, some wouldn't let you into the toilets. But she hadn't heard of anything so spectacular as a whole class rolling bottles at the teacher, or hanging a teacher out of a window by his heels.

She got up and walked down to the edge of the sea. Somehow she had to escape going to that terrible school. She took off her sneakers and waded, the wet sand squishing between her toes. Kids at home had envied her for leaving, though they thought she was crazy not to go to Europe. Mary Alice was the only one she'd told about her fears of Europe. Mary Alice never laughed at her. She defended her instead.

One day when a new kid—a "newie," as Mary Alice called them—yelled at Lynn and called her a stupid cow because she tripped over somebody's foot, Mary Alice had hit the newie. The teacher was stunned, because Mary Alice had never hit anybody before. She and Lynn and the newie had all burst into tears.

Mary Alice had tried to explain that Lynn was sensitive. "She's probably a genius."

The newie had shrieked with scorn and derision. Then after school Mary Alice had taken Lynn to the Dairy Queen and bought her a Scrump-Dilly-Ishus out of her allowance. "That new girl is a very gross person," she said.

Lynn wished with all her heart that Mary Alice were here now. If she were, it might be possible to face up to a whole school of newies. Only of course, she herself would be the newie here, and the others would be the oldies. It seemed as if you couldn't win. But if she didn't go at all . . .

She passed some fishermen's shacks. Somewhere around here lived Old Mitch, the hermity kind of old man who raised ducks and geese and liked to chase kids. She and her brothers always paid him a visit, because the boys liked to tease him a little. About half a century ago he had had a bitter feud with Grandfather Linley. One of the boys would always tell him who they were, so he would go into his long harangue about the Linley crooks.

He was there now, sitting on the steps of his little shack, tossing kernels of corn to some hens and ducks, talking to them in his high nasal voice.

Lynn approached with caution, not having the protection of her brothers. "Hello, Mr. Mitch," she said.

He slewed around and glared at her suspiciously. "Who're you?"

"Lynn Grenville. I used to come to see you with my brothers."

"Why ain't you been to see me lately?" He shooed away a greedy Plymouth Rock hen.

"I haven't been here lately."

"Off-islander, are ya?"

"Yes."

He tossed a handful of corn at some ducks. "Tell yer folks if they want to hear the real true Island stories, straight from the hoss's mouth, better come see me. I'm the last of the storytellers." He squinted his watery pale blue eyes at her. "Don't charge nothin'. Just whatever they want to put in the hat. It'll all be gone when I'm gone, and I ain't long for this shore."

A young black sheep, not yet much more than a lamb, stuck his head around the corner of the shack and looked at Lynn.

"Oh, what a cute lamb," she said.

"Cute!" Old Mitch snorted. "Eatin' me outa house and home, that critter is. Somebody left him out in the pasture in a storm. Some folks are mighty careless with their property."

"And you saved him." She stepped toward the lamb, but he did a little sideways dance.

"Charity case is all he is. Expectin' me to take care of all their stray animals. I hate a black sheep."

"Why? I think he's pretty."

"Sheep oughta be white." He glared at the sheep. "He butted me."

Lynn laughed. "Did he really?"

"Well, I'll be butcherin' him next week."

Shocked, she turned to look at Old Mitch. "Butcher him! What for?"

"Meat. What'd you think for? Anyways he's too durned ugly to live. Black! Hate a black sheep."

"Well, you're not going to enter him in any beauty contest, are you?" Lynn was outraged. Kill a sweet lamb like that!

He peered at her. "Beauty contest!" He cackled. "That's some funny."

"You can't kill him."

"Who says?"

"I say."

"Ain't your property."

"I'll tell the Humane Society."

He widened his eyes in disbelief. "Humane! Girl, you are talkin' silly. Sheep are meant to be et."

"I'll buy him from you."

His expression changed. "Don't know if I want to sell."

But she knew he did. "I'll give you two dollars for him."

"Two dollar!" He puffed up his cheeks with indignation. "Two dollar! Young lady, lamb sells for three fifty a pound."

She had no idea what lamb sold for, but she knew that gleam in his eye when he thought of two dollars cash. "Two fifty. That's my best offer." It was also half of all the cash she had. Her father would be sending her allowance next week but it wasn't much.

"I don't get nothin' but my old age check, and you, a rich off-islander, tryin' to fox me. I call that wicked."

"Two fifty," Lynn said. And she added, "He's not very big."

The old man stood up. "It's highway robbery," he said, "but I'll take it, because I hate a black lamb. It ain't natural. If the Lord was to have wanted sheep to be black, he'd have made 'em black."

Lynn had to laugh. "He did, didn't He?" She was scrounging around in her shorts pockets, hoping she had enough money with her. She had had it in mind to walk into the village, so she had stuffed some change and a dollar bill into her pockets. She counted it out. It was okay—she had almost three dollars. She put the dollar bill, four quarters, and five dimes into his dirty palm.

"Take 'im," he said. "He's yourn." He chuckled. "Probably butt you from here to town." He watched her as she walked up to the sheep, talking softly to him.

"Come on, sheep, sheep, sheep. Come on, boy."

"He's a wether. Shoulda charged you extra for the geldin'."

"Did you geld him?"

He sniffed. "Nope."

"Then why should you charge me for that?" She held out her hand to the sheep, and he stretched his neck toward her without taking a step.

"Makes him more valuable, that's why. You don't want some old ram buttin' you all over creation, do ya?"

The sheep touched her fingers with his nose. She put her hand in the black wool of his neck, and he gave a little bleat but he didn't pull away.

"Come on," she said. "Let's go." But he planted his feet when she tried to lead him. She heard the old man behind her chuckling gleefully. She took off the leather belt that she wore with her shorts and looped it around his neck. "Come on, chum." It would be a problem if the darned sheep didn't budge. She knew Old Mitch would neither help her nor give her back her money. She tugged gently, and suddenly the sheep was trotting along beside her.

"Bye, Mr. Mitch," she called back over her shoulder She had won the little battle. Now the question was, what in the world was she going to do with a sheep?

7 She walked along the shore leading the sheep. He came along docilely, except that now and then he wanted to stop for a mouthful of beach grass. She had read somewhere about sheep in Scotland that ate seaweed, but her sheep wasn't interested.

"The idea of wanting to kill you!" Lynn said. "A nice lamb like you. But you really are a problem. I'd like to tell Grandmother about you, but then she'd think she had to cope." Everybody in the family except Timothy had cautioned her not to worry Grandmother. "If we can find some place where I can leave you, I can come out every day and feed you and talk to you."

She had begun to despair of finding any kind of shelter where the sheep would be safe, when she finally came to an old boathouse that looked as if it had not been used for years.

"Let's take a look." She pushed the half-open door. Dead leaves and debris had blown up around the entrance, making the door hard to open, but Lynn pushed it far enough so a little light came in. An old dory with a rotting hull lay tipped against the wall, and one cracked oar stood in the corner. There was a small, high window with dirty glass, facing the shoreward side. Heather and marsh grass grew around the boathouse, which was built up on a piece of land that stood above the shoreline. It seemed to be above high water, but that would be something to bear in mind if there were a big storm.

Lynn broke a limb off a scrub pine and used it as a broom to get out the worst of the debris. "What do you think?" she said. "Does it look like home sweet home to you?"

The sheep leaned against her and closed his eyes with a look of bliss as she rubbed his head.

"How can I get you to stay here?" She broke off some more branches and brush and made a barricade around a patch of grass. "Will you stay here?" She broke off a little switch and shook it at him. "I don't want you wandering off and getting lost. I suppose you'll stay here as long as there's something to eat. How long will it take you to eat what's here?"

The sheep was already grazing contentedly.

"I'll get a roll of wire and make you a pen. Then you can't take off and get lost." The sheep rolled his eyes at her.

"What am I going to call you? Think I'll call you Cyrano. You're all nose." She rubbed his back and

47

scratched his neck, and then she discovered he loved to have the under part of his neck stroked gently. He stuck out his chin so she could do it again. "You are affectionate. I don't think you'd butt me. I'm going now, but don't be scared. I'm your friend. I'll be back soon."

So she had a new friend. She would write Matthew about it. He liked animals. My friend the black sheep. She laughed and felt cheered up. Maybe later, when Grandmother was used to having her around the house, Lynn would bring up the subject of Cyrano. It would be nice if she could keep him in the back yard. The only thing was, most of the yard was taken up by Grandmother's garden. Maybe he could live in the garage, beside the old Buick. Well, she wouldn't bother Grandmother about it yet.

It wasn't anywhere near time for lunch, but she was hungry, so she went to the cottage. She had rather expected to find Grandmother in the garden on a nice day like this, but she didn't see her anywhere. She looked at the garden with an eye to Cyrano's future home. Right now he'd eat everything in it, probably, but when it got colder and frost had taken what was left, a sheep wouldn't hurt, would it? Especially such a sweet sheep. She thought again with anger of that terrible old man who had intended to kill him.

Grandmother was not in the kitchen. There was a fresh-baked loaf of bread cooling on a rack. It smelled heavenly. Lynn was not used to homemade bread. She was so hungry, she could have eaten half a loaf right then. Better check with Grandmother before she ate anything, though. It was her house, after all.

Grandmother was not in the front of her house. Lynn began to feel alarmed. She tiptoed down the hall to Grandmother's bedroom. There she was, lying fully dressed on the bed with a washcloth over her eyes. She must have a bad headache, as her mother often did. Migraines, her mother said. She started to leave, but as she turned, she half stumbled and crashed into the doorframe. Just when she wanted so much to be quiet! Grandmother's eyes flew open. "I'm sorry," Lynn said. "I didn't mean to disturb you."

"Oh, that's all right." Grandmother's hair was mussed up, which was very unusual, and there was a tiny smear of dirt on her cheek. "Come in. Did you have a nice walk?" She looked pale.

"Yes, I did. Are you all right? Do you have a headache?"

Her grandmother pushed back her hair with the damp washcloth. "I did, but it's better now." She slowly swung her feet to the floor, and Lynn saw that she had on her gardening shoes. It wasn't like Grandmother to be lying on her clean bedspread with her shoes on, especially gardening shoes.

"Mother gets headaches, too. Migraines."

"Mine was nerves," Grandmother said. "I had a fright."

Lynn waited, not knowing whether she should ask what had happened. Grandmother stood up, but she seemed shaky. "Wouldn't you like to stay lying down? I could make you a cup of tea. Mother likes a cup of tea and a salt cracker when her head aches."

Grandmother sat down again abruptly and began to cry. The tears streamed down her face, but she didn't make any sound, and she didn't stop them or even try to.

"What is it, Grandma? What's the matter?" Lynn was frightened. She couldn't remember ever seeing her grandmother cry. Even after Grandfather died, the family used to say how brave Grandmother was, how she never cried in front of them.

Grandmother picked up the washcloth again and wiped her face. "There," she said, in a choked voice. "What a way to carry on." She gave Lynn a bleak little smile. "I'm sorry, dear. Pay no mind."

"Is it me being here? Do I upset you?" Lynn had to ask it, although she was afraid of the answer.

But the effect of the question was good. Grandmother pulled herself together and her eyes brightened. "Lynnie, of course not. Quite the contrary. I see I had better tell you, so you won't worry."

"You needn't if you'd rather not."

"Well, we were going to keep each other from getting

nervous, weren't we. We said that when you came. Come sit down."

Lynn sat on the bed, although she was afraid her sandy shorts would be bad for the bedspread. "I'm pretty sandy."

"Good clean sand." Grandmother glanced at herself in the mirror. "Great day! Did I look like that when they came? No wonder they . . ." She got up and combed her hair and scrubbed at the dirt on her face. "There." She sat down again. "It's Louise Small and her husband. He's a retired clergyman from the mainland. I can never remember what church it was. They are kind, well-meaning people; but I am an ornery old woman, and I hate being looked after by strangers."

"You're not ornery. What did they say?"

"Well, they came over one day in the spring, after a blizzard, to see if I was all right—and what could be more neighborly than that? Although really they aren't close neighbors. They live way over there somewhere near the golf course. Anyway I was having one of my bad days. I get through them, you know. I have ways of getting through my bad days. But they came in, and unfortunately I couldn't remember who they were. And . . ." She paused and shook her head. ". . . apparently it was late afternoon and somehow I had the idea it was morning. I was in my robe, and I invited them to breakfast." She laughed. "This crazy old woman inviting them to sit down to fried mush and bacon and grapefruit at five o'clock in the afternoon.

They were alarmed. They had the doctor sent to me. Not even my own doctor, poor man. There was quite a fuss all around, and since by that time I had my senses back, I was, I'm afraid, not terribly patient with any of them."

"They should mind their own business," Lynn said. She felt angry at these people who had humiliated her grandmother.

"But they were doing good. It's so hard to deal with people when they are determined to do good."

"Were they here today?"

"Yes. I was working in the garden. They have an idea, a very well-intentioned, kind idea, which I will have no part of." She ended the sentence on a rise of anger, and then checked herself. "They have my welfare at heart. But by the great Lord Harry, as your grandfather would say, I can attend to my own welfare."

"What is their idea?"

Grandmother waited a moment. Then she spoke as if she had to force the words out. "They want me to go to a home for old women."

"No!" Lynn was shocked. "They can't do such a thing. You've got your own family."

"I've always said I'd never live with my children, and I never will."

"Grandmother, those people can't make you go to a place like that. They aren't even related to you."

She sighed. "I don't know. I have nightmares that they could. Force me to, or get the children to come after me. If they decided I was incompetent . . ."

"But you aren't incompetent."

Grandmother looked at her sadly. "Sometimes I am, Lynn." Then she spoke with her old forcefulness. "But darn it, I know how to handle it."

"Did you tell them I was here?"

"No. Somehow it felt dangerous. They might say I wasn't fit to look after you."

"That's ridiculous." Lynn felt uneasy, in spite of her attempt at sounding sure. "If you do have to tell them about me, why don't you say I'm here for a visit. Anyway it's true—I *am* here for a visit."

Grandmother got up and smoothed the bedspread. "What a mess I've made here. Well, dear, would you like some fresh bread and wild plum jam?"

"I'd love it." Lynn followed her grandmother to the kitchen. Somehow she had to protect her grandmother from nosey busybodies. And herself, if she wasn't going to school.

8 When she got up in the morning, she found Grandmother out in the garage looking at the old family bicycle.

"I thought we could get new tires and get this thing fixed up," she said, "but I'm afraid it's too far gone. Goodness, it must be twenty-five years old. I think it was Edith's."

"I remember Matthew used to ride it when we were here."

"Yes, all the boys did. But it's rusted up." She gave it a little kick. "What we'll do is, we'll go into town and get you a new one."

"That would be wonderful. But I don't want you to spend money on me. Mother said you were not to."

"Your father gave me far more for your board than I need. We'll use some of that money. You need a bicycle. We'll go into town as soon as you've had your breakfast."

Lynn was excited. It would be wonderful to have a bike. For one thing she could get out to see the lamb much more easily.

After breakfast, Grandmother started up the old Buick. There were almost no cars on the road, but she drove slowly.

"My reflexes aren't what they used to be," she said. "I take it slow and easy. When I was a girl, I was known as a fast driver. Never had an accident, though, never once in my whole life." Sand had blown onto the road in small windrows. She shifted down to a lower gear. A milk truck tooted its horn, and the driver passed her with a wave. "One of the Starbuck boys," she said. "Jim, I think it is. Or Jake."

She found a place to park in front of the Old North Church. "We can walk over to Young's and see what they've got."

As they walked down the street, she put her hand on the small of Lynn's back. Automatically Lynn straightened up. Her mother scolded her for slumping. But Grandmother only said, "You're going to be as tall as I am."

If she could only be sure of looking like Grandmother when she was a grown-up, she'd feel a lot better. She stopped and put a letter to Matthew into a mailbox. She had written him asking him whether people really could make Grandmother go to a home. If he didn't know, he'd find out.

Outside the bicycle shop stood an old-fashioned bike with a big front wheel and a small rear wheel. Grandmother began a conversation with the man in the shop. "She wants a good one," she said, "but that doesn't mean it's got to be a twenty-speed thing or anything like that."

The man smiled. "How about a five-speed? We've got some Schwinns here. You can't beat a Schwinn. Or there are some beautiful Peugots, but they run a little more."

Grandmother looked around. "Schwinn, Peugot," she said shaking her head. "In my day you ordered something from Montgomery Ward for fifteen dollars and put it together yourself."

"Putting a bike together is a chore, Mrs. Linley," he said. "You don't want to mess with that. How about this blue Schwinn? Do you like that one, young lady?"

"Oh, yes," Lynn said. "It's beautiful."

"Has it got a guarantee?" her grandmother asked.

"Oh, sure thing, Mrs. Linley. Year guarantee. If anything goes wrong, you bring it right back to me."

"Yes," Grandmother said drily. " 'Course it would be a whole lot better if nothing went wrong."

"I'm sure it won't. Do you want to try it out, young lady?" He wheeled it out onto the sidewalk. "Careful of the cobblestones."

She rode slowly and bumpily over the cobblestones of the street. It was a fine bike. "I love it," she told her grandmother.

"Very well. We'll take it."

"You want me to charge it, Mrs. Linley?"

"Now, Harold," she said, "you know I don't charge things." She opened her purse and slowly counted out the money. "Is that right? You'd better count it."

She had given him five dollars too much. When he had given it back and given them the guarantee and the instruction book, they set off, Lynn pushing the bike. She tried to say thanks, but Grandmother brushed her off.

"Your father's money," she said. "I called that young man Harold, but I'm not so sure he isn't Eddie. Now I think of it, he's about fifteen years too young to be Harold." She shook her head. "Terrible thing to lose your memory."

Most of the people who were not tourists knew Grandmother and said good morning. Some stopped to chat, and when Grandmother introduced Lynn, she said, "My granddaughter is visiting me." She didn't say she'd come to stay.

They stopped at the outdoor flower market, and Grandmother bought some gladioli, and then they moved on to a pickup truck where boxes of vegetables were on sale. The owner wasn't there, but there was a scale and a sign that said, "Weigh your own and leave money in the box. Thank you." Grandmother weighed out some potatoes and tomatoes. "Had terrible luck with my tomatoes this year," she said to a tourist in shorts who was buying apples. The tourist commented on the trusting nature of the merchant who left people to pay for their purchases.

"Well, I suppose it wouldn't be practical in a big city," Grandmother said. "But this is Nantucket."

The girl who owned the produce came back with a styrofoam cup full of coffee. " 'Mornin', Mrs. Linley," she said. "Find what you want?"

"Yes, thanks. This is my granddaughter."

The girl nodded. "Howdy. Got a new bike."

"Yes." Lynn felt like the little girl she had been when she used to trail around town after Grandmother four or five years ago. Then she remembered how tall she was, and her shoulders slouched.

They stopped at Mitchell's Book Corner so Grandmother could pick up a copy of *The Eustace Diamonds* that she had ordered. "I'm working my way through Anthony Trollope," she said. "I've got forty-two books to go. Lynn, you find yourself some books."

Lynn picked out a collection of science fiction short stories and a book by Rachel Carson about sea creatures. When they left the bookstore, Lynn waited on one of the wooden benches while Grandmother went up the curved steps of the bank, holding to the iron railing.

Lynn ran back to the vegetable truck and bought a bag of lettuce and parsley for the lamb, and tucked it under the books in the bike basket.

Grandmother came out and said, "You can ride your bike. We'll just put the flowers and things in the car. I hope that bike is all Harold said it is. Or whatever his name is."

As soon as Grandmother had gone, Lynn set off for the lamb's boathouse. She hoped he was all right.

It was a good bike. She had never had a multiple-speed bike before. She sped past half a dozen other cyclists, and could almost have caught up with Grandmother if she had wanted to.

She got off the main road after a while and pedalled along a rutted sandy lane that was hard going. The sand was hard to ride in. She got off and pushed the bike. She went by a row of small, weatherbeaten houses, some with rowboats hauled up in front. At one house a boat had been filled with geranium plants. She liked the look of the red blossoms against the silvery gray of the old boat. Grandmother said the salt air raised the old ned with cars and electrical appliances and things, but it sure made wood look pretty.

She walked as fast as she could, eager to see her lamb. And then she was at the boathouse and there was Cyrano, still eating. But he had pushed his way through the flimsy barricade of boughs and was cropping the grass on the other side.

She put the brace down on the bike, got the bag of lettuce and parsley, and ran up to him. "Hi, Cyrano. How you been? I missed you." She put her arms around his neck and hugged him. He smelled good. She sat back on her heels and began to stroke his face. As he had done yesterday, he stretched out his neck so she would scratch his throat, and he closed his eyes in a look of such sheer bliss that she had to laugh.

"I brought you some store-bought food. I suppose

you'll eat it all up in one mouthful." She looked around. "You've made a lot of headway here. I'm not going to be able to keep you here long." She opened the bag and fed him the lettuce and parsley from her hand. He munched eagerly. "Do you know the difference? Is it any better than the wild stuff?"

When he had eaten it all, she took him for a walk down the beach, wheeling her bike along the hard sand. As long as she scratched his head and neck every few minutes, he walked at her heels as if she were his object of greatest devotion. "Anyway I'm nicer than Old Mitch, aren't I?" she said.

She sat down on an overturned dory and looked at the sea. There were half a dozen sailboats in the harbor. It was a good sailing day. The fresh wind whipped her hair around her face. The sheep settled down to eating the grass that grew in clumps down on the beach. Overhead the sky was the same silvery gray as the old boats and the houses. A green heron flew past, his wings slowly beating the air, and the usual collection of gulls settled down close to Lynn to see what she had to offer.

"Sorry, you guys," she said. "Nothing for you." She lay on her back and looked up at the sky for a while, and then she got her book from her bicycle basket and read. One of the science fiction short stories was about an enormous bee that an old man kept as a pet. The bee annihilated a nosey social worker that insisted upon opening the closet door where the "pet" was kept. How nice it would be to have a bee like that who would take care of disagreeable people.

Cyrano settled down beside her, his legs neatly tucked under him.

"You have cute knees," she told him. "I have terrible knees. All bone and joint. In the winter they get chapped."

A fisherman in hip boots waded along the shore a short distance from them and cast his line. "He's fishing for blues," Lynn said. Matthew always fished for blues when he was here. She hoped he would get her letter quickly. In the village Grandmother had seemed to be perfectly all right, except for getting the bike man's name wrong. Maybe I'm worrying more than I need to, Lynn thought.

It was hard to worry on such a beautiful day. She watched a yacht sailing out past Tuckernuck Island. It would be nice to be rich and have a yacht. And be composed and cool and a gracious hostess, dealing out little sausages on toothpicks and glasses of dry sherry on the deck, standing straight and tall and making witty conversation. A storm would come up and she would be very brave and calm, and tell everybody what to do. Her beautiful chiffon caftan would be ruined by the waves and her hair would be wet, but she would look noble like the carved ship's figurehead at the Seven Seas gift shop.

"My grandfather's family has lived here for one hundred and fifty years," she told Cyrano. He lifted his head and looked at her with soulful eyes. "Your ancestors probably knew my ancestors." She put her arm around his woolly neck and buried her face in his wool. He gave her a soft little bleat and nuzzled her neck.

She got up. "I'd better go home for lunch. Come on. I'm going to fix you a different grazing ground. You eat so fast." She brushed the sand from her bike and together they went up the rutted road to the boathouse.

9 Days of beautiful weather slipped by uneventfully. Grandmother seemed better, although once in a while she called Lynn "Ella," and a couple of times she seemed surprised when Lynn came into the house. But nothing more than that. The letter came from Matthew, saying he didn't think anyone outside the family could force Grandmother to go to a home "unless she was really in bad shape." Lynn worried a little over that part of the sentence and then put it out of her mind because Grandmother was not in bad shape.

"She could live with us if necessary," Matthew said. "Don't worry about it. Have you had a look at your new school yet? Don't let them scare you. Strangers are only people you haven't gotten to know. If you have any problems, kiddo, just drop me a line. I don't know if I'd be much use, but I'm sympathetic! Love, Matt."

Well, it was nice to have his sympathy. But it wouldn't help her face those kids. She wondered what he would do if he knew what she was planning.

The letters that came from Belgium were full of enthusiasm. Even Timothy was enjoying himself. Lynn shared the European letters with her grandmother, who had her own as well, but the letter from Matthew she kept hidden.

Lynn went out to see her lamb every morning, unless Grandmother wanted her to go into the village with her, and that didn't happen often. The lamb had grazed his way methodically all around the boathouse area, and Lynn had moved him to the edge of the moor. One day she found him quite a long distance from where she had left him, among the heather and scotch broom and bearberry. The next time she went into town, she bought a long rope and an iron stake. Because she was afraid the rope would chafe his neck, she wove a scarlet and blue collar for him out of some old scarves that she found in the attic. Grandmother said she could have them. The scarves had too much stretch, however, and she finally found a wide leather strap that worked better. Cyrano was very sly about pulling out of the scarf collar, but Lynn had enjoyed making it. There was something especially wonderful about making something for someone you loved, and Cyrano was marvellously non-critical.

Several times the week before Labor Day she rode past the school, struggling with herself about what to do. One day she even lay down her bike at the edge of the walk and went up the wide steps. Her father always said doing a thing wasn't as hard as anticipating it. But as she reached the door, half a dozen girls, older than she was, burst out, almost crashing into her. She jumped back, and they ran across the grass. One of them tripped over Lynn's bike and said, in a loud voice, "What a stupid place to leave a bike!" She turned and glared at Lynn. "Whoever left a bike there," she said in the same unpleasant voice, "ought to be arrested."

They ran off down the street, and Lynn picked up her bike and rode slowly home. No way could she go to that school.

On the day after Labor Day she awoke early with the painful realization that school started that day and she wasn't going. Grandmother had mentioned it a week ago, but she seemed to have forgotten it again. Lynn put on a clean pair of jeans and a clean white shirt and her nylon windbreaker and then made herself a sandwich, as she often did, for lunch. She left the house after breakfast, just as she would if she were going to school. Leaning on the handlebars of her bike, she looked up the road that led to school. Then she rode out to the moor where Cyrano was tethered. He was always glad to see her and didn't expect anything of her but love.

She felt very guilty, but not so guilty she could change her mind. Staying away from the house and going home only when she was pretty sure school was out, seemed sneaky. And she kept thinking how shocked her family would be. Still, it was something she could do, and going to school just wasn't. That night when she got home, Grandmother didn't mention school, but Lynn worried about it, even after she'd gone to bed.

The next day she rode her bike over to the school in the middle of the morning. She ought to be able to make herself go. It was terrible cowardice not to. Her father would be disappointed in her. And Matthew was sure to ask about school in his letters and when he came for Thanksgiving. She hated herself for being such a coward. But as she looked at the building, she heard voices faintly through the open windows, and she pictured a teacher being hung by his heels. If they would do that to a grown-up teacher, what might they not do to her? She shuddered. She knew they wouldn't like her.

The weather held. And she continued to spend her days with Cyrano. Sometimes in the evening Grandmother asked how school was going, and Lynn, feeling guilty, would say, "Fine," and change the subject. In order to sound as if she were in school, she mentioned the few names she knew—Susan and Patty Coffin, Biddy Sondheim. There were so many Coffins on the island that Grandmother had no way of knowing which Coffins these were, making it fairly safe. She had heard of some Sondheims, but she didn't know them. When she asked the name of Lynn's homeroom teacher, Lynn said it was a hard name to say, let alone spell, but the woman was from the mainland. That was answer enough, since Grandmother wouldn't know a teacher from the mainland.

I am getting to be a terrible liar, Lynn thought. And she hated herself. "What a tangled web we weave when first we practice to deceive," her mother used to say. It was true.

Answering questions about what she was studying was easier. Using Grandmother's library card, and going to the library after school hours, she checked out a lot of books on subjects that she would have been studying at her own school. And she set herself to doing a certain number of hours of organized study each day, taking books with her when she and Cyrano spent their days at the beach or beside one of the freshwater ponds.

She read *Macbeth* and *Othello*, and liked them so much she went on a Shakespeare spree for several weeks, even reading late at night after she was in bed.

She found some out-of-date biology textbooks and studied them, making notes. They were old, but she thought maybe biology didn't change all that much. She studied the French conversation book that Sam had given her, and talked French to the ducks on the pond or to the gulls or to Cyrano.

"You've got a French name," she told him. "How's my accent? J'aime, tu aimes, il aime, nous aimons, vous aimez, ils aiment."

Cyrano poked his nose into the hollow of her elbow.

"Does that mean I'm good or terrible?"

She couldn't find a math book in the library, but that didn't worry her. She had never had any trouble with math.

One book she got had things like Washington's Farewell Address to His Troops, and the U.S. Constitution, Bill of Rights, and Declaration of Independence. She came to the conclusion that Jefferson was a lot better writer and speaker than Washington. The Bill of Rights, she thought, had some relation to Grandmother's problem.

Because she spent so much time at the ponds, she became interested in the birds, and began a systematic study of the kinds of ducks at Gibbs Pond and Maxcey's Pond, making notes about their colors and habits. Sometimes she lay on her stomach in the warm grass and peered at the perch and bass and pickerel.

There was seldom anyone around, except an occasional lonely fisherman.

One day when the fog rolled in, Lynn rode into the village and spent a long time at the Whaling Museum on Steamboat Wharf. The next day she checked out *Moby Dick*.

When the weather cleared again, she sometimes left Cyrano to his own devices and rode over to the other villages: Wauwinet, where she sat on the porch of the empty Casino and read and ate the sandwich she took with her every day; Quidnet, Coskata Beach, 'Sconset. Everywhere there were so few people, she almost thought of the island as all her own. The rutted cross-island roads were empty, and now with the early frosts, the beach plum and wild grape, the blackberry, wintergreen, and heather were vivid colors. Always the white rollers coming in off the sea fascinated her. She thought she could never find a better home.

But on the day that she rode over to look at the Hidden Forest, the weather changed suddenly. She was sitting reading deep in among the swamp maples and the beeches and thick ferns when she felt the sea-change. The sun disappeared, and a chill fog rolled in. It was hard to see. At first she thought she should stay where she was until the fog lifted, but after a while, when it showed no signs of going away, she cautiously began to feel her way out.

She was not on a path. All she could do was to edge her way carefully through the forest, trying to find

open land. Once she fell over a tree that angled across
her way. Bruised in the shins, she got up, trying to get
the damp leaves and cobwebs out of her face. The
woods, which had been so pleasant when it was sunny,
seemed sinister now. She thought of hidden pirates and
robbers and strange animals, although she knew very
well there hadn't been a pirate for years, and the only
animals of any size on the island were deer. But then
she thought of snakes. Were there poisonous snakes on
the island? She had never seen any, but that didn't prove
anything. It was best to step quickly, not let her feet
rest long in any one place.

How would she ever find her bike, even if she got
out? She had left it leaning against a tree at the edge of
the woods, but she had lost her sense of direction entirely.

Well, one thing at a time, as her father liked to say.
Just get out of the woods. Then she could look for the
bike.

The fog drained the color out of the ferns and left
the trees leaning against each other like tired ghosts.
A wind riffled the leaves with an eerie rattle, and
moisture began to drip silently. When she put her hand
on a trunk to steady herself, she drew it back quickly,
repelled by the slimy wetness.

Fear made her tired, drove her to fighting the branches
and leaves blindly, in mounting frustration. She seemed
to be getting nowhere. What were you supposed to do

when you were lost? Stand still and try to control your terror? She ought to stay still till the fog lifted. But it might not lift for days. She remembered old stories of the island getting socked in for a week at a time, planes unable to land, life at a standstill. No, standing still wouldn't do.

As she stepped forward, trying not to think about snakes, something flapped violently almost in her face. She gave a cry and fell back against a tree, trembling. Then she heard the hoarse hoot of an owl. Scared to death by an owl! She was ashamed of herself and moved on.

She tripped over a downed branch and fell heavily. For a moment she was too discouraged to get up. But the cold, wet ground was unpleasant. It was astonishing that a place that could be so warm and sunny and friendly at one moment could be so menacing and dark and evil the next. She got up and plunged on.

For all I know, she thought, I might be going in circles. If she had a knife, she could blaze a trail, the way they did in the northwest. But she didn't have a knife, and anyway the fog was so thick, she'd never see the blazes.

She pushed hard to move a heavy branch that was in her way. It gave with a sudden crack that made her stumble forward so that the twigs scratched her face. When she picked herself up, she was in a small clearing that looked familiar, but so had a lot of other places in the last half hour; and none of them had led to anything. She paused for a moment, and suddenly within a dozen feet of her a wraith stepped into the clearing. It was tall and slender, half masked by branches, gray and unsteady in the fog. There was nothing it could be but a ghost. She screamed and plunged off in a different direction. Faintly behind her she thought she heard a voice cry, "Hey!" But that must have been the wind. Ghosts didn't say hey.

She was shaking and crying as she fled through the trees, heedless of the branches that hit and scratched her. And then all at once she was out of the woods.

She couldn't believe it. Her knees gave out and she sank to the ground, shivering and trembling in the chill wind. It was a long time before she got up to look for her bike. And when she did, it was because she was not sure, after all, that the ghost of the woods would stay in the woods. She skirted the trees, looking for her bike, and in a miraculously short time found it. It was not quite where she had left it, though. It had been standing against a beech tree, but now it was lying on its side. Well, maybe the wind knocked it down. Grateful for it, she wheeled it back to the road and started home.

She was going to have to tell her grandmother the truth. A girl didn't stumble into the house from school, soaking wet, torn, scratched, and shaken.

Grandmother was in the living room, reading. She looked over her glasses and then half got up. "Gracious goodness! What happened?"

"I got lost in the fog in the Hidden Forest."

"Oh, you poor child." Then for a moment she looked puzzled. "Isn't it a school day? I lose track . . ."

"Yes, it is." Lynn took a deep breath. "I didn't go to school, Grandmother. I've been cutting school."

Grandmother gave her a long look. Then she said, "Ah, well. Nantucket out-of-doors in Indian summer is hard to resist. But I wouldn't cut too often, dear. You'll get behind in your work, and they might get cross."

Lynn opened her mouth to explain that it wasn't just one day she was cutting, but all the time. "I . . ." Her eyes filled with tears, partly at her own wickedness in deceiving Grandmother, partly in reaction to the horrible experience in the woods.

"There, there," Grandmother said. She came and put her arm around Lynn's wet shoulders. "You just pop into a nice hot bath, and I'll make you some tea and cinnamon toast. I've been in those woods myself when they were pretty spooky. But you're all right now. Run along and get warm and dry."

And so, again, Lynn didn't confess.

10 One morning when she went out to see Cyrano, he was gone. The collar, which had worn through from his constant rubbing against it, lay on the heather still attached to the rope, but the rope was wound around the iron stake. She had found him several times tangled up in the rope and had tried to teach him how to reverse himself and unwind. "Like a maypole," she told him. But Cyrano hadn't understood about maypoles, and he went on getting the rope wound uncomfortably tight. This time the collar had broken.

There was no sign of him anywhere. She rode along the path where she often led him, but no Cyrano came galloping up to her to get his throat rubbed. She called and called, but the cry of the gulls was the only answer.

On a hunch, she rode over to Old Mitch's place. It didn't seem likely that Cyrano would make his way back there, but just in case, she would look.

Old Mitch was chopping firewood. With the hatchet still held over the block, he turned his stiff shoulders so he could see who it was.

She started to ask if he had seen Cyrano, but at that moment she heard the lamb bleat. "He's here! Where is he, Mr. Mitch?" She could hear the lamb, but she couldn't see him. His voice seemed to come from the other side of the shack.

"Did what?" Old Mitch said. His face was blank. "Who?"

"My lamb. He must have gotten loose and come back here." She started toward the importunate bleating.

"No lamb of yourn here." Old Mitch brought the blade of the hatchet down on the chopping block and left it quivering. "No property of yourn here, young lady."

But Lynn went around the corner of the shack and there was Cyrano tied on a short tether, stretching out his neck toward her. "There you are." She rubbed his head and reached for the rope to untie it. "What did you run off for? I hunted and hunted . . ."

"Here, what you doin' there?" Old Mitch looked more disheveled and disreputable than ever, and Lynn could believe what her brothers said, that he bought his clothes in the Madaket dump. He was wearing jeans much too big for him, held on with a rope around his waist. And over his soiled shirt he wore a torn sleeveless jacket of the kind that Nantucket calls a wammus. "Don't you monkey with my sheep."

Lynn looked at him indignantly. "He's not your sheep. He's mine."

"Heck he is. That critter's mine."

Exasperated, Lynn stamped her foot. At once Cyrano

began to stamp his foot. Lynn wanted to laugh, but this wasn't the moment. "I bought him from you. Don't you remember?" For a second she wondered if everybody on the island was losing their memory. But then she saw the glint in Mitch's shrewd little eyes, and she knew he was trying to put something over on her. "This is my lamb, Mr. Mitch. I paid you two fifty for him, if you remember. And I guess you do, all right. So I'll take him along now. Thanks for looking after him."

She relaxed her hold on the rope and put her hand deep into the wool on Cyrano's neck. "Come on, Cyrano."

Old Mitch blocked her path. "I'll have the law on you if you steal my sheep."

She raised her voice as if he were deaf. "I am not stealing your sheep. I am taking my own property." In her mind she apologized to Cyrano for calling him "property," but you had to talk to Old Mitch on his own terms.

"Found him out on the moor, half-starved."

"When?" she said, thinking he meant the first time.

"This mornin'. Half-starved and all tangled up in some fool rope."

She patted Cyrano's plump side, and the lamb nuzzled her arm. "Does he look starved? Please get out of my way, Mr. Mitch." She was beginning to wonder what she would do if he didn't give up the lamb. She was determined not to go without Cyrano. A little uneasily, she glanced at the hatchet, with its blade sunk in the stump. Was he kooky enough to get violent?

But as she advanced on him, Old Mitch took a step backward. "I'll have the law on you, stealin' my sheep. We don't hold still for sheep stealin' on this island. This ain't America, y'know. This here's Nantucket."

"I know that, Mr. Mitch. Excuse me." She almost had to step on his toes to get past him.

He was muttering as she went to her bike and walked away, balancing it with one hand and leading Cyrano with the other.

"Who're you?" he yelled. "Who're you that's stealin' my sheep? What's yer name?"

"Grenville," she called back.

"Where you live?"

"Boston."

"Where you live on the island?"

She pretended not to hear him.

He followed her a little way, waving his fist. "Gonna have the law on ya. You can't escape me."

She told herself he wasn't really frightening—just a slightly crazy old character, or maybe just eccentric. He didn't know who she was, and he couldn't get at her, even if he meant to. But she was concerned about where to keep Cyrano so that he'd be safe.

Because she couldn't think of any other place, she

went to the boathouse. Cyrano had cropped the grass right down to the dirt; if she left him here, she would have to get him some food somewhere else. She sat down on the sagging sill to think. Cyrano sat beside her with his head on her knees. "What am I going to do with you?" she said. He rolled his dark eyes up at her trustingly. "All right, I'll think of something." She rubbed his head thoughtfully. "I guess I'm going to have to tell Grandmother about you and see if you can come home. The garden's about shot now, after that early frost. I can stake you out where you won't get into trouble." She looked into his dark eyes, but he wanted to nibble her nose and she found it very hard to be serious. "You've got a real knack for getting into trouble, haven't you." She got up. "Right now I'll get you a bunch of stuff to eat that ought to last you overnight, and I'll leave you here till I can talk to Grandmother."

She let him come along with her while she pulled up armfuls of marsh grass and everything she could find that looked edible. She had to bop him lightly on the nose to make him stop eating what she had already picked.

The coarse grass cut her hands, and the roots went clear to China. "What I go through for you," she told him.

At last she put him in the boathouse and piled up the forage just outside the door. The sky looked dark, and

77

there was a rising wind. She walked along to the waterline to look at the sea. Long combers showed white on the gray water far out. She noticed some of the red kelp, or whatever it was, that Cyrano was so fond of. She gathered some of it and ran back to the boathouse with it. "That's for dessert. See you tomorrow." She gave him an extra hug. "It's blowing up a storm, so stay inside."

By the time she got home, it had begun to rain. She came in through the back door and found Grandmother in the kitchen making pies. She looked younger and more herself than she had since Lynn had come.

"Afternoon, dear. How was school?" That was the first time she had asked a direct question about school, although she had said things like "how did the day go?" and "is everything going all right?" and "what did you learn today?"

"Fine," Lynn mumbled. She fled to the back hall to hang up her jacket and to avoid questions about school. "The pies smell wonderful."

"I'll tell you a secret," Grandmother said, wiping her floury hands on her apron. "Today is my wedding anniversary."

"Really?"

"Yes. Your grandfather and I would have been married fifty-two years if he'd lived." She leaned her elbows on the sink and looked out the window. Then she gave a little sigh and turned around. "You think it's a funny

78

thing, me celebrating with pies and all kinds of collations, but your grandfather and I promised each other years and years ago, no matter who went first, the other one would always mark our anniversary with love and joy." She brushed a lock of hair back from her forehead. "I will admit to you, it wasn't possible those first few years after he went. I couldn't do a thing but shut myself up in my bedroom. But the third year, I had a talk with myself. 'Look here, Doris,' I said to myself, 'you're breaking your word to the one you love the most. You pull yourself together now, and do what you promised.' So I cooked up a good dinner, the way I did when he was here. Pies, hot rolls, rib roast, the house all shining and ship-shape, and the best linen and dishes out. Yellow roses in the cut glass vase. And a bottle of wine. And I sat down to my dinner right at nine o'clock, when I heard the Portuguese bell starting curfew. When the wind's this way, you know, you can hear it from the South Tower. We'd toast each other on the first stroke, and then he'd . . ." For a moment she hesitated. ". . . he'd kiss me, and then when the fifty-second stroke had sounded, he'd say grace and thank the Lord for our wonderful life together." She took a deep breath. "So I make myself remember all I've had to rejoice in." She took a pie out of the oven. "I hope you like berry pie. It's your mother that doesn't like it. Always said it made her teeth turn blue." She laughed.

"Grandmother, if you'd like your anniversary dinner by yourself, I can eat early . . ."

"No, I think it will be lovely to have you with me. But bless you, you'll starve to death before nine. Why don't you make yourself a nice sandwich?"

"No, I'd rather wait."

Lynn wanted to tell her how beautiful she thought the anniversary celebration was, and how brave she thought Grandmother was, but she didn't know how to say it. When Grandmother turned away from her, Lynn went up from behind and put her arms around her. Grandmother didn't say anything, but she put her own arms over Lynn's and held her tight for a moment. Then she picked something off Lynn's sleeve and turned toward her, holding it up. It was a little piece of the red kelp.

"Dulse," Grandmother said.

"Oh. I guess I got it on me at the beach." She caught her breath. She was supposed to have been in school, not at the beach.

Grandmother held it up to the light. "The fronds look like little hands, don't they. They build up, you know, layer on layer. It's good to eat."

"For people?"

"Yes. In Scotland they say 'he who eats of the dulse of Guerdia and drinks of the wells of Kildingie will escape all maladies except black death.' " She held it under the faucet in the sink to wash it off and then ate it.

"There. Barring the black death, I'm safe." She opened the oven and looked at her roast. "We're having quahog chowder first, in your special honor. Your grandfather was not much of a hand for clams, although he went wild over scallops."

"I can hardly wait." Lynn went upstairs with her head full of wonderful smells and expectations and her heart full of an unsettling mixture of joy and sadness. It had never occurred to her before that the same things could be happy and sad at once.

11   The first note of the bell came to them faintly on the wind. They stood facing each other across the candlelit table. Grandmother lifted her sherry glass, and her eyes looked very bright. Lynn didn't know exactly what to do with the tiny liqueur glass of sherry that Grandmother had given her. She'd never been involved in a toast before. She lifted it, wondering if she should say anything.

"To the memory of our happy life," Grandmother said softly. She made a little upward gesture with her glass, and Lynn did the same. Then Grandmother took the first sip of her sherry, and Lynn did the same. Then they sat down.

While the bell bonged out its slow fifty-two strokes,

as it did every night at nine, they sat silently, sipping the sherry. There were bowls of hot chowder in front of them, and Lynn thought she was going to faint with hunger.

The whining of the wind around the house drowned out the last few strokes, but Grandmother was counting them in her mind. She put the glass down and bowed her head. "Thank you, Lord, for Aaron Linley and our children and our children's children and our happy lives. Please protect my children and theirs from harm. And although I grow forgetful, let me never forget the good things you have bestowed upon me. Amen."

When she looked up, there were tears in her eyes but her voice was gay. "Now then, you are dying of hunger. Eat, my dear, eat!"

And for some time Lynn was so busy eating, she could hardly talk at all, but she didn't think Grandmother minded. Her mind seemed far away, although not in the forgetful, absent way—just preoccupied with her thoughts.

When at last they had finished the pie, Lynn smiled at her grandmother. "Are my teeth blue?"

"Not by candlelight," her grandmother said. "Candlelight makes everything what it ought to be and just a smidgin better."

They cleared the table and did the dishes, and as she was carefully wiping one of the plates, it occurred to

Lynn that she hadn't broken anything of her grandmother's at all except one everyday water glass that had
slipped out of her hand.

"Grandmother," she said, "do you like sheep?"

"Sheep?" Her grandmother looked over her shoulder
at her, her hands still in the soapy dishwater. "Sheep?
Yes, sheep are all right. Always getting into things, of
course, but not as bad as goats. There used to be seven-
teen thousand head of sheep on this island at one time.
Not many left now. Lambs are sweet little things. I used
to like to walk out and see them in the spring." She
dumped the dishwater and rinsed out the pan. "Do you
remember your grandfather at all?"

The moment had gone by to tell her about Cyrano.
"Yes, I do. Mother says I couldn't, because I was so
young, but I do. He took me for a ride in a pony cart."

"Yes." Grandmother looked pleased. "That was John
Tolliver's pony. I've got a picture of it somewhere."

They went into the living room and she lit the fire.
She opened a drawer in the desk and rummaged around.
"Here's some of the old pictures." She sat beside Lynn
on the sofa and began to turn the pages of an old album.

There were faded snapshots of Grandmother and
Grandfather when they were young, wedding pictures,
pictures of children and grandchildren. Grandmother,
identifying the different people, forgot John Tolliver's
pony cart.

83

"Here I am at about your age," she said. "That was high school graduation, I think. A little older than you are."

Lynn took the picture in her hand and stared at it a long time. It looked familiar. "You almost look . . . almost look like me," she said. She couldn't believe it, there was such a strong resemblance.

"Yes, I've always thought you favored me the most of any of them."

Some loose pictures fell out into her lap. "Here I am with my first bicycle. I think I was ten. Oh, how I remember that bicycle. I'd been pestering my father for two or three years."

Lynn held that picture alongside the high school one.

"And this must be the prize in the family collection." Grandmother laughed and held up a picture of two very young children, a boy and a girl, sitting in a tin washtub. "That's your great-uncle Bob and me."

Lynn studied the three pictures and looked at her grandmother. It was the first time she had ever even thought of Grandmother as being any age but elderly.

"It's strange, isn't it," Grandmother said, "Those three creatures and this one sitting here, and they're all me."

"I was just thinking that," Lynn said.

Grandmother chuckled. "You always thought of me as an old lady."

"Not an *old* lady. Just my grandmother."

"I know. The thread of time. That's what holds our

selves together, and each of us to the other members of the family. The thread of time is mysterious and strange." Grandmother sat quietly for a few minutes, looking through the pictures. In the lights and shadows cast by the fire, her face looked young, the lines hidden, the outlines softened.

Lynn tried to remember herself at early ages and then to imagine herself grown-up, middle-aged, old. She had an eerie feeling, as if time streamed away from her in two directions at once, and she stood precariously on a rock in the middle of that turbulent stream. It made her feel dizzy.

Grandmother was looking at a picture of herself in her wedding gown, holding a bouquet of roses. She closed her eyes and leaned her head back. The picture slipped from her hands. She seemed to have fallen asleep, although her eyelids fluttered a little.

Lynn sat still, watching the dancing flames in the fireplace and trying to think about time passing and what it meant to be alive. It was very hard to get hold of.

A log broke apart with a small crack. Grandmother sat up abruptly and opened her eyes. "Oh, my," she said. "Must have dozed off. Better get to bed, dear. Your father may want you to go out and help him with the cranberries in the morning, if that storm dies down." Without looking at Lynn, she got up and left the room, turning out the lamp as she went.

Lynn sat still. It had been many days since Grandmother had mistaken her for her mother. *Help your father with the cranberries.* Grandfather had owned a cranberry bog a long time ago.

Absently she picked up the iron poker and poked the log apart so it would burn out. She replaced the fire-screen and went upstairs to bed. She lay awake listening to the quiet sounds of Grandmother moving around her bedroom below Lynn's, and after the sounds ceased, she still was unable to sleep. If only Grandmother wouldn't lose her memory. If only there were some sure way to protect her. She longed to be able to talk to her father or Matthew. It seemed a long time until Thanksgiving. She thought about writing to her father, but if she did, her mother would be alarmed and come rushing home. All that would do would be to upset everybody. She knew Grandmother would not go to live with her children. She had said so a hundred times.

The wind screamed at the windows, and somewhere at the back of the house, a shutter banged. Lynn wondered if they were going to have a hurricane. If it was still so stormy in the morning, she would go get Cyrano and put him in the garage. She had almost told Grandmother about him. Tomorrow she would for sure. If everything was all right.

12 When Lynn came downstairs in the morning, the wind was blowing hard. Branches of trees were strewn about the garden and in the road. Although she was later than usual, there was no sign of Grandmother.

She tiptoed to her room and saw that she was still in bed. She wasn't sure in the dim light whether she was awake or not. Softly she said, "Grandmother?"

Her grandmother stirred. "I have a headache," she murmured. "One of my bad ones."

"I'll get you a cold cloth."

She brought a washcloth that she held under the faucet and then wrung out. She put it gently on her grandmother's forehead and felt her shiver. "Have you taken any aspirin?"

"No use," Grandmother said in the same faint voice. "Dear, will you get me the brown bottle in the medicine chest? And a glass of water?"

Lynn got them, but when she opened the bottle, it was empty. "They are all gone."

Her grandmother groaned. "Forgot to get it refilled." She winced with pain and put her hand to her head.

"I'll go to the drugstore and get some," Lynn said.

"Is it storming?"

"Not bad. I'll go right away. Will you be okay till I get back? Do you need anything?"

"No, just one of those pills. It's a migraine . . ." Her voice trailed off and she turned her head to one side.

"I'll hurry."

Lynn put the bottle in the pocket of her parka and hurried outside. The forces of the wind almost knocked her over. She could never ride her bike in this. She pulled the drawstring on the hood of her parka, bent her head into the tearing wind, and set out on foot.

It was slow, hard going. The wind, when it gusted, almost knocked her over, and every few minutes she had to stop and turn her back to it so she could get her breath. Trees were bent almost double.

Boughs broke off and sailed through the air as if they were as light as twigs. A gull over her head beat his wings desperately, not moving ahead at all. Then he gave up and fell to the earth like a scrap of paper.

Sand stung Lynn's face and got into her eyes and down her neck, and the blown salt spray made her lips sting. Keeping her eyes almost closed, she slogged along in the middle of the rutted road.

She passed a cottage closed up for the winter and saw the upstairs shutters banging askew in the wind. One of the windowpanes had been shattered. She noticed the name on the mailbox. Ault. It must be that doctor's place. She would tell someone when she got to town. If she ever got to town.

Her chest hurt. An extra strong gust of wind almost knocked her over. She clung to a fencepost a few minutes. If Grandmother weren't in such pain, she'd give it up, but she couldn't bear to go back without the medicine. Grandmother's face had been so pale and drawn.

She let go of the post and stood up. For the moment, at least, the wind had suddenly died down. She could see the oily, brown, heaving water of the sea. Some kind of small shore bird lay dead near the road.

She took a breath and hurried along to take advantage of the lull. She kept thinking of Cyrano. As soon as she could, she'd go get him, but right now he was probably better off in the boathouse. If he **had** sense enough to stay there. And if high water didn't get to him. She glanced anxiously at the sea. The tide was out, but she could hear the surf smashing all along the shore. She remembered her father saying that Nantucket had no bedrock. She wondered if it could just collapse and fall into the sea.

She struggled on, slipping and almost falling in the loose drifts of sand. A clump of seaweed blew with a slapping sound against the shoulder of her jacket. She thought of Grandmother's dulse.

The storm door on another summer cottage was banging loose. She beat her way up to the porch, forced the door shut, and shot the bolt. No telling whether it would hold. She sat down for a moment on the steps to rest. While she sat there, a Jeep passed her. She jumped up and waved her arms, but whoever was driving didn't see her. He probably could hardly see out of his windshield. Even the windows on this protected porch were scarred by the blowing sand.

She pulled herself together and trudged down the road. Concentrating on taking step after difficult step, she was surprised when she finally found she was on the outskirts of the village. A big elm leaned into the street as if it might fall at any minute. She hurried past it. The streets were littered with branches, debris, the contents of blown-over trash cans. A small English sportscar blocked the sidewalk, slewed around by the force of the wind. If this is a hurricane, she thought, I'll have a neat story to tell when I get back to the mainland.

Someone looking out of one of the houses, rapped on the window and motioned for her to come in, but she waved and kept going. A couple of cars passed her, driving very slowly. There were no pedestrians anywhere.

"Everybody but me," she muttered into the hood of her parka, "has got enough sense to stay in."

Some of the shops had put up shutters, some had boarded up their windows, or made big X's of tape across the glass. A few had lights burning, but most were deserted. A man in yellow oilskins came around the corner and beat his way toward Steamboat Wharf. Maybe the Harbormaster. There was bound to be a lot of damage to small boats.

If the drugstore wasn't open, she would telephone the emergency number on the bottle. She wasn't going to go back empty-handed, not after all this.

But the store was open. The man behind the counter had a raincoat on over his white jacket, as if he were about to leave. He looked up in surprise when she came in.

"What you doin' out in this wind, sister?" he said.

"I had to get some pills for my grandmother." She fished around in her pocket for the big bottle. "Is this a hurricane?"

"This is what the weather bureau calls a whole gale. Just one step away from a hurricane." He looked at the bottle. "Mrs. Linley?"

"Yes."

"Mrs. Linley out to Madaket?"

"Yes," she said, a little impatiently. What was so great about its being for Mrs. Linley?

"You didn't walk in here all the way from Madaket, did you, sister?"

"Yes," she said. "My grandmother's got a bad head-ache."

He frowned at the bottle. "This prescription is three years old."

"It can still be refilled, can't it?"

"Not without getting a refill from a doctor."

"Can't you call him?"

"Doc Jacobs has been dead more than a year."

For a moment Lynn thought she was going to burst into tears. She couldn't go back to Grandmother without the pills. "Can't some other doctor okay it? She's got a lot of pain."

He shook his head slowly. "Don't know if anybody would do that without seeing her first, and nobody's going out in this storm for a headache."

"It isn't just a headache," she said. "She's in bad pain. It's a migraine. She's an old lady, you know."

"Yes, I know Mrs. Linley. Well, you hold on a minute, and I'll see what I can do." He looked at her closely. "You must be half-froze." In a minute he came back from a little room in the rear of the store and handed her a cup of coffee. "Tuck that into you. I'll call around. Providing the phone lines aren't all down."

She waited, sipping the hot coffee and relaxing a little in the warmth of the store. She could hear the druggist's voice, but not what he said. It seemed a long time before he came back.

"Can't raise any of the doctors," he said. "Most of the telephones are out of order."

"Can you tell me where the nearest doctor lives?" she said. "I'll go see him."

The druggist took down a big bottle from one of his

shelves. "Tell you what I'm going to do. I'm going to give you four of these pills. Shouldn't do it. I could get in trouble for it. But I guess this is kind of an emergency. You tell your grandmother when she feels better, she should go see a doctor. I know she went to Doc Jacobs for years, but he's gone now, and she ought to have somebody. At her age, she needs looking after." He shook four tablets into a small envelope, wrote directions on it, and handed it to Lynn.

"I really appreciate it," Lynn said.

"All right. I was just about to close up. You come on out back, and I'll drive you home."

"You don't have to do that."

"Come on along. Can't have you blowin' out to sea. The Coast Guard's got enough trouble without looking for you." He led her out the back and opened the door of the four-wheel drive. The step was high, but he said, "Guess you can make it with those long legs."

He turned up the collar of his coat and climbed in beside her. "That was some mornin' stroll you took." He glanced at her sideways as he started the engine. "You one of the Linley grandkids?"

"Yes." Here we go with the questions, she thought, but he had been so nice, she couldn't be rude. "I'm visiting."

"You Ella's girl?"

"Yes."

"Heard Ella'd gone across the water for the winter."

"Yes."

"That's nice. I was over that way myself during the war. Italy and Morocco. Where's Ella?"

"Belgium."

"Never got to Belgium myself."

"Which war were you in?" She forced herself to ask, not because she cared but because she wanted to be civil.

He looked surprised, and then he laughed. "World War II. I'm not hardly old enough for that other one."

She felt foolish. That was how it always turned out. "I'm very ignorant about history."

He didn't say much of anything else because he had to give his attention to keeping the car on the road.

"Do you live out Madaket way?" she asked, after a long silence. It seemed like a safe question.

"No, I live over to Wauwinet."

That was the other end of the island. He'd really gone out of his way for her. She wanted to tell him how grateful she was, but she was still trying to think how to put it when he pulled up in front of Grandmother's. She just said, "Thanks an awful lot."

"You're welcome. Hope your grandmother feels more chipper. She's a nice lady." He reached across her and opened the stiff lock on the door. "Run in now, before you blow out to sea."

She ran to the house while he waited to see that she

got in all right. She waved and went inside, the door slamming behind her.

"Is that you, Ella?" her grandmother called.

"It's me, Grandmother. Lynn." She went into the room. "I brought your pills."

"Oh, I'm so glad." Grandmother lifted herself up a little and took the pill and the sip of water that Lynn gave her. "I was worried. I heard the wind. You're all right?"

"Fine. The druggist brought me home."

"He's a nice man." She lay back on the pillow, looking very white. "It will begin to work in a few minutes, and I'll probably sleep awhile. You get warm and dry. Thank you, dear. You're such a comfort." She reached out and patted Lynn's hand. "Dear Lynnie." She closed her eyes.

Lynn ran upstairs and got out of her clothes. She took a shower as hot as she could stand it, and then she came downstairs in her robe and built up a fire in the fireplace.

She had a peanut butter and jam sandwich and sat close to the fire. Now that it was all over, she felt rather pleased with herself. She'd done something right at last. Grandmother had needed her, and she had come through. The only trouble was, now people would know that "Ella's girl" was living on the island and ought to be in school.

13 Grandmother was in the kitchen, singing, when Lynn came downstairs next morning. She was wearing a bright blue apron that made her eyes look very blue, and she was just taking a pan of johnnycake from the oven.

"You feel better," Lynn said.

"Yes, indeed. I almost always feel fine the day after one of those silly headaches. Pour yourself some orange juice, dear, and sit down. I was just remembering one time your grandfather decided some sea air would clear my head after a bad headache so he got a friend of his, I think it was Oscar Smith, to take us sailing in his boat."

"Did it work?"

"Like a charm. I felt wonderful. But your poor grandfather was seasick the whole time." She laughed. "He always told that story on himself. He could laugh at himself, your grandfather could. I don't think any of my children inherited that trait. Or perhaps it has to be learned. I don't know." She cut a generous piece of johnnycake, buttered it, and put it in front of Lynn. "The bacon's almost done."

Lynn was wondering whether she could laugh at herself, and decided she couldn't. She'd have to work on it, and maybe she could laugh at criticism. Maybe someday she'd even laugh at her silly fears.

"I never should have let you out in that high wind. I didn't realize until I found sand in my bed this morning. Then I turned on the radio and got the news. Sending you out in a hurricane for those old tablets!"

"It was what they call a whole gale," said Lynn proudly.

Grandmother shook her head. "It could have been dangerous. We should have phoned the drugstore. Joseph would have come out."

She was glad they hadn't thought of that because then she wouldn't have had the chance to act heroic. She told Grandmother what the druggist had said about getting a new prescription.

"I don't want a new doctor," Grandmother said. "Old Dr. Jacobs understood me. I'm sure the other men are very good, but I don't know them."

"But I don't think the druggist will give you any more of those pills. He said he shouldn't have given you any."

"Poor Joseph. He's so conscientious. Well, I don't get those headaches more than once or twice a year, and one tablet usually takes care of it, so perhaps my little supply will last me."

Lynn looked at her quickly. Did she mean last her for

the rest of her life? She put the unpleasant idea quickly out of her head.

"Do you like Dr. Ault?"

"The Boston boy? Oh, yes, he's a nice boy."

"Maybe when he comes down, he'd give you a prescription for some new pills." It worried Lynn to remember the pain in her grandmother's face and to think she might be without her pills sometime, perhaps when she was all alone.

"Well, if I think of it, I'll ask him sometime."

Lynn suddenly remembered the broken window at the Ault house and mentioned it.

"Oh dear," Grandmother said. "They have some lovely antiques. I hope they weren't ruined." She poured some coffee. "Let's see. I think the Jacksons have their key. I'll call Mrs. Jackson and tell her." She put on her glasses and looked up the number. "I hope the lines are repaired." She dialed. "Mrs. Jackson, this is Doris Linley. My granddaughter tells me there's a window broken at Dr. Ault's place . . . Yes. They've got some nice antiques. . . . Yes, terrible storm, wasn't it. I'm fine, thank you. No, no damage here that I know of." After she had hung up, she said, "George will see to it. I hope the furniture is all right. Did it rain?"

"No, but there was a lot of sand and salt spray blowing."

Grandmother looked out the window. "Trees are

down. And my garden is a mess. Well, the frost got it first and I'd had the good of it for this season."

"Grandmother," Lynn said and stopped.

"What is it, dear?"

Lynn took a deep breath. "Would you mind very much if I kept a lamb in the garage?"

"A lamb in the garage?" She looked surprised, and then she laughed. "That takes me back. Nobody has asked me a question like that since my boys grew up. 'Mother, can I keep a centipede in the Mason jar?' or 'Mother, can I have a goat?'" She laughed again. "I've missed it."

"Then it's all right?"

"If you'll take care of it."

The telephone rang. Because she was worried about the sheep, she decided to go get him right away. Grandmother was still talking on the phone when Lynn put her parka on. She was speaking in such a formal, polite way, Lynn suspected it might be those people who were always trying to look after her.

She waved and went out the back door. The wind was blowing, but compared to yesterday it was light. The surf was heavy, and the beach and the road were littered with debris from the ocean and the land. Lynn wanted to hurry, but she had to ride carefully to avoid being spilled off by the soft sand or unexpected junk in the road.

The tide was in, higher than usual. She was relieved to see the boathouse still standing, as she came up over the last rise. She got off her bike and ran, calling Cyrano, but he was nowhere in sight. The food she had left him was gone. She looked at the surf that pounded on the sand such a short distance away, wondering how high it had come during the storm. She felt panicky. There was some seaweed at the door of the boathouse, but she couldn't tell whether it had blown there or had been left there by waves. She touched the sand; it was hard and damp.

She began walking in widening arcs, calling and calling for Cyrano. A German shepherd bounded up to her, and she remembered that dogs were likely to kill sheep, if they got a chance. She shooed the dog away angrily, as if he were already guilty.

She trudged through sand and grass and moor for almost half an hour, not finding her lamb. It was useless to look for hoofprints because the wind had blown everything around so much.

Out near Jackson Point, she came to a small, neat, shingled cottage, with vines growing over the back porch. About to go around it, she heard a bleat.

"Cyrano?" It seemed unlikely that it was he.

There was a clatter of hoofs on loose boards as the black lamb galloped across the porch and down the steps. He ran up to her, butted his head on her stomach and held it tight against her for a long time.

She hugged him. "Where have you been? I've been hunting everywhere."

The door of the shack opened, and a man with a grizzled beard looked out. He wore a faded Navy watch-cap on the back of his head. "Your sheep, is he?"

"Yes. I'm sorry he bothered you. He ran away."

"Sheep will."

"Thank you very much."

The pale eyes peered at her. "What for?"

"Well, you didn't drive him off, or—or butcher him or anything."

"Butcher him!" The man laughed. "I'm a fisherman, not a butcher. And I couldn't drive him off. He wouldn't go."

"He was probably scared, in the storm."

"He wasn't the only one. Bad storm."

"Yes."

"Well, take him home then." He went back into the house and shut the door.

Lynn ran down the path with Cyrano at her heels. She wandered off toward one of the ponds, surveying damage on the way. It was cold and windy by the pond, but she settled with a book in a sheltered place. She supposed the school had been closed yesterday, but it surely would be open today. She sat until midafternoon, and then she took Cyrano home.

"You're going to stay in here with the Buick and my bike," she told him, opening the garage door. "I'll get you some food. After a while maybe you can graze in the garden. In the meantime, don't nibble on the awnings or knock over the flowerpots or anything like that. You've got to make Grandmother like you."

When she shut him in the garage, he bleated piteously and raked the door with his front feet. "Stop that, Cyrano," she said. "I'm going to get you some grass and stuff." She ran into the house and got the Scout knife that she had inherited from Sam. Grandmother was vacuuming in the front of the house. Lynn didn't stop to talk. She wanted to get Cyrano fed so he'd stop banging on the garage door.

She went across the road and began to cut grass and shadbush and anything green she could find. When she had filled the bushel basket she'd brought along, she took it back to him. He was still bleating as if his heart was broken. But as soon as his nose found the basketful of feed, he stopped his crying and began to munch happily.

"There, that will hold you for a minute, I hope. Don't strew it all over. Grandmother is a tidy person." She kissed the top of his head and went into the house.

Before she had a chance to ask Grandmother to come and meet Cyrano, Grandmother said, "Dear, we're out of milk. Would you mind going for some?" She handed Lynn some money. "The little market in Madaket will do."

Lynn got the bike out of the garage. Cyrano looked up at her, a long strand of grass hanging from his mouth. "You are a glutton," she said, and she wheeled the bike outside and closed the door.

At the store she discovered that they also sold pet food. She got out some money of her own and bought five pounds of alfalfa pellets for Cyrano. If they were good for guinea pigs and rabbits, they should be good for sheep. Anyway Cyrano was definitely not a picky eater.

"How's Mrs. Linley?" asked the woman who waited on her.

It had been ridiculous to hope that she could avoid notice in such a small place as Nantucket Island. Sooner or later people were going to say, "How's school?"

And as she was thinking it, the woman said, "How do you like school on the island?"

"Oh," Lynn said, "I like everything. I mean, I really enjoy Nantucket." She felt her face getting hot.

"Nice for your grandmother to have you here."

That was the end of it for that time. She left her bike on her back porch and put down the alfalfa pellets. In the kitchen she put the milk into the refrigerator. Grandmother was lying down. Lynn went back to the garage and put the pellets out of Cyrano's reach. Let him finish off the browse first. Then, because she was tired, she went upstairs and flopped on the bed.

She was just dozing off when she heard her grandmother's voice. It sounded frightened. She ran downstairs to find Grandmother in the hall, looking bewildered.

"I really must be losing my mind," she said in a faint voice.

"What's the matter?"

"I could swear . . . Lynn, I could swear that there's a sheep in my kitchen."

Lynn clapped her hand to her head. "How could he?" Then she seized her grandmother's hand. "No, no, you're not going crazy. There probably *is* a sheep in the kitchen. Remember, I told you I had a lamb . . . I asked you if I could . . ."

A look of immense relief spread over Grandmother's face. "You did. Oh, you did. It had slipped my mind entirely. Oh, what a relief. I really thought I had lost my mind."

"But he isn't supposed to be in the house. Oh, gosh, I don't know how he got out. Or in. I'm so sorry. I had him in the garage." Lynn was on her way to the kitchen, with Grandmother behind her.

There stood Cyrano in the middle of the floor, a spilled bag of flour spread around him, solemnly chewing on a long piece of uncooked spaghetti.

"Cyrano, you bad sheep!" He had spoiled everything. She'd have to get rid of him now.

Cyrano looked at her with his bright, mischievous eyes, and then he came over and butted her gently in the stomach. Grandmother began to laugh and laughed so hard, she had to sit down.

Lynn was still saying how sorry she was and trying to sweep up the spilled flour.

"Don't worry. It will only take a minute. Sheep always get into everything. I'm so relieved. I really thought I'd gone right round the bend." She laughed again, and her low, happy laughter finally cheered Lynn.

"I don't know how he got out of the garage, or in here."

"Sheep are like goats. They can open doors that would stop a first-class burglar." She reached out and rubbed Cyrano's neck. He came closer and put his head in her lap. "He's a sweet one."

"I won't have to give him up?"

"Of course you won't. What's his name?"

"Cyrano."

Grandmother laughed again and stroked his nose. "Very good. I like you, Cyrano. You're all right."

Lynn could hardly believe that Grandmother would let her keep him. She even seemed to be happy about it. "I'll make sure he doesn't get out again."

"He doesn't want to be cooped up. Let him have the run of the garden. He'll clean it up for me. Where did you find him?"

"I bought him from Old Mitch."

"Abner Mitchell? He probably cheated you."

"He thinks I cheated him."

"Abner always thinks that."

"I had to buy him, because Old Mitch was going to butcher him."

"Yes, he would have done it too, for the meat. You did right to buy him. Well, Cyrano, you can't stay in here, but we'll make you welcome in the garden. Come along, boy." She led the sheep outside. "What is that?" She nodded at the bag.

"I got him some rabbit pellets."

Grandmother smiled. "Rabbit pellets. Well, why don't you save those for a rainy day. Meanwhile, he can start on the carrots. He won't mind if they're frost-bitten. There's a tin pail in the garage you can use for water."

With a broad smile on her face, Lynn went to get the pail. You just never knew how things were going to turn out. All that worry about Cyrano, and here was Grandmother happy as a lark over him. Everything was going to be fine.

14 The weather turned foggy. Great rolls of dense, dripping fog spread in from the sea. Occasionally a plane could be heard overhead, trying to find a rift so it could land, but usually it had to fly away to Hyannis, and after the first two days, flights were cancelled altogether. The seven o'clock boat sat outside the jetties all one night, with a dozen impatient passengers aboard, before it ventured to nose its way cautiously past Coatue Point. The golf courses were deserted, cars drove very slowly with their lights on. Flying low overhead, the gulls wheeled and cried out. And in the background, like disconsolate ghosts, the foghorns moaned.

She had to go somewhere. It was too miserable to stay outside. She had avoided going to the library during school hours, in case the librarian got curious. But today she took the chance. She settled herself in a corner, and did some coughing so the librarian would think she was out with a cold. She finished Melville's *Omoo* and wrote a book report on it, just the way she'd have to do for school. Maybe some day it would come in handy. If she ever got up courage enough to go to school again.

At noon she bought an ice cream and tonic water (a soda at home) at the Sweet Shop, and then wandered along the waterfront in the fog, thinking about the old whalers.

She turned onto Straight Wharf. On one side were the summer shops, shuttered now and insubstantial in the mist. On her other side was the invisible water, and the closely-packed fishing boats, whose superstructures seemed to float unsupported.

At the end of the wharf, she leaned against a piling. The fog made her feel dreamy. She listened to the bell buoys out there somewhere in the water.

A voice said, "Who are you?"

She started. It was a ghostly voice. She could see no sign of anyone. Clearing her throat, she said faintly, "What did you say?"

"Who're you?"

There was no one in sight. "Where are you?" Her own voice sounded hollow.

"Right in front of you, silly." A long figure made of mist unwound itself from the stern of a dory that was pulled up onto a float just below her. The figure leaped up onto the wharf and turned into a tall, thin boy, about fifteen years old.

Lynn's fear turned to anger. "What'd you want to scare me to death for?"

"Didn't set out to scare you," he said calmly. "I just asked who you were. Perfectly friendly question."

"I thought you were a ghost."

"Sometimes I am." He sat on one of the pilings,

dangling his long legs. "When I'm down here, I'm a ghost."

"There's no such thing."

"Then how come you thought I was one?"

"Well, it's just an expression."

"I believe in ghosts," he said. "Who are you anyway?"

"My name's Lynn Grenville, if that's what you want to know." She felt irked still that he had scared her like that.

"Are you from America?"

"Of course, I'm from America. I'm *in* America."

"You know what I mean. America is over there." He studied her. "Why aren't you in school?"

"Why aren't you?"

"I've got a disease."

She took a step backward. "What kind?"

"German measles."

"Oh, that. I've had that."

"You can have it again. This makes my third time."

"It's nothing much."

"Why aren't you in school?"

"Because I don't want to be."

"Who does? You can't go by that."

"I'm not going to any school," she said fiercely, "where they hang teachers out the window by their feet."

He gave a little laugh of surprise. "They don't do that."

"I heard that they did."

"It might have happened years ago."

"And I suppose you'll tell me they don't drum you out of the regiment if you don't go along."

"That's just the girls."

"You may not have noticed, but I happen to be a girl."

"Hey, you are, at that. You're so tall, I thought you might be somebody else."

"You're rude." She tried to see his face in the fog. "You sound familiar. Do you ever hang around the Hidden Forest?"

"Where the ghost goeth, nobody knoweth."

"Whose ghost do you think you are?"

"I'm myself. A hundred and fifty years ago I was first mate on a whaling ship."

"What," she said skeptically, "not captain?"

"I was working up to it. But I was lost when a whale upset the longboat."

She wanted to be scornful, but she was impressed, too. He sounded so matter-of-fact, as if it were real. In the dense fog, anything seemed possible. She thought of the different versions of her grandmother at different times in her life. Maybe that could work for reincarnation. "What was the name of your ship?"

"The *Pequod*."

"Now I know you're a fake. That was the ship in *Moby Dick*."

"This was the *Pequod II*."

"And I suppose your best buddy was Queequeg."

"Of course not. Queequeg is a fictional character."

She peered at him, trying to see his face more clearly. He was not smiling. She felt confused.

"We were one of the last whalers to go out. The harbor began to silt over in the 1850's and after a while we couldn't get in, even with a camel."

"Camel!"

"Of course, I'm talking about a nautical camel. Besides, in 1854 some mainlanders began to produce kerosene and they didn't need whale oil anymore. We made our last voyage in '62. That's when I was washed overboard."

"This is a weird conversation."

He shrugged.

"If you stay out there, you'll get something worse than German measles." She felt it necessary to say something sensible. "It's cold right through to your bones."

"Not to an old salt," he said. And as she turned away, he called after her. "You can come to school if you want to. I won't let them drum you out of the regiment."

She looked back but already the fog had swallowed him up. "What's your name?" she called.

His voice sounded hollow. "Call me Ishmael." And the words were lost in the dense mist almost as soon as he called them out. A gull swooped past her, shrieking mournfully, and the foghorn gave its hoarse cry.

She went back to the library and looked up the word "camel" in the big dictionary. After the animal definition, it said, "also a nautical term for a cradle on pontoons designated to lift ships in shallow water."

She saw the librarian looking at her, and she remembered to cough. As she left, the woman said, "Better stay home with that cold in this weather, dear."

She walked home slowly. There were no ghosts. At least not a ghost that was also a live person at the same time. Or were there, and she hadn't heard about it? He was either a person she thought she'd like to know, or he was a person she'd detest, or he was really a ghost and not a person at all.

At dinner she said to her grandmother, "Do you believe in ghosts?"

"I've learned over the years not to say flat out that I don't believe in something. And I guess if there were ghosts, you'd find them on Nantucket."

Lynn went outside after dinner to make sure Cyrano was all right.

He bounded up to her and waited to have his throat rubbed. "You got enough to eat?" she asked him. "I can hardly see you. Good thing you're black. If you were white, you'd look like a ghost lamb." On her way back to the house, a rabbit leaped in front of her and disappeared in the fog. "Shoo," she called after him. "Stay out of Cyrano's supper." Her grandmother had said there were deer around, but she hadn't seen any yet.

She stood a moment on the back steps feeling the damp, wraparound sensation of the fog, and then she opened the door and went in to the warm reality of Grandmother's kitchen.

15 The fog kept up, with an occasional short break. She explored the Peter Foulger Museum, and the Maria Mitchell Library. She wandered around Old North Wharf, Commercial Wharf, Straight Wharf, Swain's Wharf, and Old South Wharf, until she was, she told herself, a card-carrying bona fide wharf rat. She examined the Old Gaol, and she memorized the compass that told how many miles it was to Tahiti, Hong Kong, Berlin, Moscow, Daytona Beach, and a lot of other faraway places. I am stuffing my head with useless information, she thought. But she found a big old atlas among Grandmother's books and read all the facts she could find about the places mentioned on the compass. At dinner she would discuss some of these things with Grandmother, feeling like a terrible deceiver because she knew Grandmother thought she was talking about her schoolwork. She really enjoyed talking to her, though, except for that uneasy feeling.

Grandmother knew a lot, especially about botany and biology, which had been her field in college.

One evening Grandmother said suddenly, "Lynn, about school . . ." and paused.

Lynn caught her breath. Here it comes. She felt like bolting out of the house.

"Am I going to have to go to the PTA?"

Relieved, Lynn said, "Oh, no. Of course not. There's no reason why you should."

"Oh, I'm thankful for that. Your mother used to complain bitterly if I didn't go. I never enjoyed it. The only suggestions I had were always frowned upon by the others, and I got so I'd just sit there like a stupid lump." She went on to talk about something else, and Lynn relaxed.

The next day she went around and around the block where the school was, trying to make herself go in and register. The deception was getting to be too much for her. She worried about it all the time. And yet, once she started she'd have to keep on, no matter how dreadful it was.

It was lunch hour, and the yard was full of yelling kids. As she watched, two of them ran up to the chain link fence and peered at her. She had the feeling she was the one enclosed, that they were looking at her the way you look at animals in the zoo.

"So you're back." It was Susan, with Biddy Sondheim.

Not sure what she wanted to say to that, Lynn said nothing.

"You'd better clear out," Susan said rudely. "We are sick of off-islanders. We've had it right up to here with off-islanders." She made a graphic gesture across her throat. A volleyball bounced near her. She grabbed it and ran.

"Don't mind her," Biddy said. "She just flunked a math test. She's in a foul mood." She lingered, studying Lynn curiously. "Are you going to school here or what?"

"I don't know," Lynn said. "It depends." Then as Biddy started to leave, she said, "Did you ever . . . you know . . . roll those bottles at the teacher?"

Biddy gave her a mocking little smile. "Wouldn't you like to know." She ran off.

Lynn pedalled her bike slowly along the fence. The bell rang, and kids lined up in a long, pushing, impatient line. Somebody just behind her on the other side of the fence said, "Look sharp, mate." It was Ishmael. He loped off toward the school building, his long arms and legs swinging. She wasn't even sure he had been speaking to her.

That night at dinner, she said to her grandmother, "Was Ishmael a real person?"

"You mean the *Moby Dick* Ishmael? No, I don't think so. Although the story is based on a real whaling vessel, the *Essex*, that sighted a white whale and was rammed and sunk by it. All hands were lost except a few men who drifted in a lifeboat for months. That gift shop in town that has the figurehead, that was Captain Pollard's home at one time. He was master of the *Essex*."

"Did you ever hear of a ship called the *Pequod II*? An old whaling ship?"

"Can't say I did. But there were a lot of ships in those days." Grandmother passed her delicious corn relish to Lynn. "Try this. New batch. Did you feed your rabbit tonight? He seemed hungry."

"Rabbit?"

The little worried frown appeared on Grandmother's forehead. "I don't mean rabbit. What am I saying? What do I mean?"

"Oh, you mean the lamb. Yes, I gave him some pellets." To keep Grandmother from worrying about being forgetful, she said, "There *is* a big rabbit that comes around all the time. He got into the pellets."

"This is a rabbity island. Your uncle Jim always wanted to shoot them, but I wouldn't hear of it. Though they do raise the old ned in a person's garden." She took up her work again.

Lynn went outside to talk to Cyrano. He was sitting contentedly with his feet tucked under him, chewing. She talked to him and played with him for about ten minutes.

When she came inside, she said, "Guess what! There's not a shred of fog. The stars are shining."

"Good. A person gets sick of fog." Grandmother put down her work, and they went together to stand on the back porch. "It's warmed up, too. Maybe we're in for some more Indian summer. Although you can't tell. We could get socked in again by morning." She turned to look at Lynn. "Is tomorrow Sunday?"

Lynn stopped to think. "Saturday."

"Would you like to go clamming?"

"I'd love it." Lynn had never been clamming. Her brothers had always said she was too little.

"Well, I like to go early, just before sun-up. You'll need warm clothes and old ones because they'll be a mess. I imagine there's some boots here that'll fit you." She opened a closet where about a dozen pairs of rubber boots were stacked. "All sizes. You find some you can wear."

Lynn found boots that fit, more or less. She was excited about going clamming, and she could see that Grandmother was, too. She'd lost her tired, worried look.

"If you can stand a cold breakfast, I'll put a little collation together to take with us, to save time in the morning." She already had the aluminum foil out and was packing her delicious coffee cake, made that morning, and fresh baking powder biscuits spread with wild plum preserves. "We'll take the Buick and go over to the other side of the island. It's your father's secret clamming ground, but he gives me custody when he's away." She got the Thermos bottle and set the coffee pot on the stove. Lynn began looking for the picnic basket.

By the time they went to bed, both of them were in high spirits.

Lynn had thought it would be hard to get up in the dark, but expectation had already waked her when Grandmother knocked on her door. She dressed quickly in the cold darkness. Downstairs she found Grandmother in a pair of Grandfather's work pants, a heavy sweater with a hole in the elbow, and hip boots. She had pulled her hair back into a knot and tucked it under somebody's old fishing cap, and had already packed the breakfast hamper and the clamming gear into the car. There were buckets, rakes, small wooden floats, and a ball of twine.

The good weather held. As they drove down the 'Sconset Road, the dark sky began to lighten. It was cold, but the wind was down.

As they went through the village of 'Sconset, Grandmother pointed out the big arrow sign that said, "THREE THOUSAND MILES TO SPAIN."

There was not a soul to be seen in the street, and no lights in the shingled cottages.

"Do you know the poem Bliss Carman wrote about 'Sconset?" Grandmother asked.

"Did you ever hear of 'Sconset where there's nothing much but moors?
And beach and sea and silence and eternal out-of-doors."

They were in sight of Sankaty Head light before Grandmother turned down a short, bumpy track and stopped the Buick near the shore.

After the days of fog, the clear air seemed astonishing. They could see the eight beams of the Sankaty light, on the other side of the golf course, blinking their steady on-and-off as they had done since 1848, reaching out thirty miles to sea.

The rising sun turned the water to steel. Some distance out, a big sailing boat seemed on fire in phosphorescence. Grandmother pointed out a marsh hen in the sandy cove. On the rocks, two gulls squabbled over mussels.

Grandmother got the gear out of the car. "We ought to find plenty of clams. They'll be two or three inches under, and it's messy business because the bottom is black mud. Sometimes you can feel 'em with your feet and then you can get them up with your rake, but if you can't do that, you just have to dig in with your hands." She opened the picnic basket. "Better eat a bite before we begin." She handed Lynn a slice of coffee cake and poured coffee from the Thermos into two mugs. "Only time I like my coffee black is when I'm clamming."

Lynn leaned against the car eating the good cinnamon-flavored coffee cake. "What are all those little boats?"

Grandmother shaded her eyes and looked out at the water. "Scallopers. Goodness sake, is it that late in the season?"

Lynn got the binoculars and looked at the boats. She had never been here late enough in the season to see scallop boats. "What are they dragging?"

"Dredges. They tow six dredges made of chain link, to get the scallops."

"How do they get them aboard?"

"Well, if they're lucky, they've got a power winch. More than likely they'll haul them in by hand. Then they'll dump them onto a culling board and somebody—probably the fisherman's wife—gleans out the whole mess. It's mighty hard work." She took the binoculars to look at the boats. "Scallops must be scarce. Usually they don't have to move out of the harbor for a few weeks at least. In time they'll have to work their way around to Madaket."

"Can we get some scallops?"

"Only off-season, and then you're allowed only a

bushel for a family a week. You can't use boats or dredges."

"How do you get them?"

"Walk along looking at the bottom through a glass or plastic box, and when you see some, you haul them up with a rake. But by the time you've shucked your bushel basketful, you've hardly got enough for one mess. It's not worth it, to my mind. Abner Mitchell will bring us some. He always does."

"I thought he hated Linleys."

"He likes cash." She rinsed out her coffee mug in the seawater and hung it inside the hamper. Next she fastened the tops of her hip boots. "Ready for the fray?"

Lynn took one of the buckets and a rake and waited to see what Grandmother would do next.

Grandmother waded into the cold water. Lynn shivered and stepped in after her. Because of the Gulf Stream, the water off Nantucket was never as cold as she thought it would be, but on the first of November, it was not exactly balmy. Lynn's boots sank into the thick black ooze, and it took an effort to pull each foot loose. Grandmother filled her bucket with water and placed it on the bottom, marking the place with a float attached by a string to the handle of the bucket. Lynn did the same thing.

She moved out slowly behind Grandmother, and when Grandmother stooped and felt around on the bottom, Lynn did too. But all that she found at first were broken shells and small rocks.

"Feel for the hinge," Grandmother said over her shoulder.

Lynn stepped into a hole in the mud and cold water seeped in over the top of her boot. She shivered. Grandmother thought catching scallops was hard work. What did she think clamming was? But she couldn't complain; she had wanted to come. Besides, it would be fun to write the family about it. She moved her hand around on the muddy bottom, stirring up black, bad-smelling ooze. Her hand was very cold. But she felt something that might be a clam. She got her rake under it and brought it up. "Grandmother, look!"

Her grandmother looked back and smiled. "Good work." She seemed pleased. "There'll be more. Put it in your bucket."

There were a lot more. Lynn forgot, at least to some extent, how cold she was. Grandmother too was raking them in almost as fast as she could reach for them. She seemed able to locate them with her foot, but Lynn found she had to crouch and feel around with her hand. But they were there, all right.

The sun came out, brilliant in a cloudless sky, and between the sun and the exertion, she stopped shivering. She filled one bucket and got another.

By the time Grandmother signalled a halt, they had a good-sized catch.

"I've got to quit," Grandmother said. "Not as spry as I used to be." She put her hand on the small of her back and winced. "But we got a good mess of them, didn't we? We'll have steamers for supper, and tomorrow I'll fry up some. They'll taste good." She poured some more hot coffee for both of them.

Lynn was so proud of herself, she could hardly stand it. All her early life her brothers had said she was too little to do things right, and then when she grew, they said she was too big, too awkward, for practically everything. Wait till Timothy heard about all the clams she'd dug!

She lifted the pails into the trunk of the Buick, which left her hands cold and wet and smeared with muck. She ran back to the water's edge to wash them off, as Grandmother had already done.

Grandmother stood for a moment looking far out to sea. "I guess if you grow up on an island, it seems like home to you, but I've never got over the strangeness of it, set down way out here in the ocean." She pointed to a gull that flew up and then dropped his mussel on a rock. As it hit and the shell cracked, he dove down to get it.

"Smart fisherman," Grandmother said. A duck with white patches on his black head flew low toward some inland pond. "Skunkhead coot," she said and got into the car.

Lynn laughed. "Is that really its name?"

"Nickname. It's proper name is surf scoter."

Grandmother knew a lot of things. If I don't get back to school, Lynn thought, I'm not going to know anything. For sure next week I'll register. But then she wasn't really sure she would.

When they got home, they took the clams out of the car and put them on a big worktable in the garage so Grandmother could shuck the ones she wanted to fry.

Grandmother looked up at the cloudless sky and said, "Fog before evening."

16 Grandmother had been right about the fog. It began coming in long thin gray streaks soon after they got home. By the time they had the clams finished, the fog had become what Grandmother called, "a regular old peasoup."

She had insisted that Lynn change out of her wet jeans and socks before she helped with cleaning the clams, but she herself was still in muddy old pants, which she had rolled to her knees.

"No sense my putting on anything clean for this job. As soon as it's done, I'll pop into a hot bath."

She pushed a strand of hair back with her hand. Her

face was mud-streaked and her hair awry, but Lynn thought she looked beautiful. Her eyes were alive and amused. All she needs, thought Lynn, is to be having a good time.

Grandmother wiped her hands on her big apron that was tied around the wet and muddy trousers. "Shoo, Cyrano," she said, pushing his nose away. "Sheep don't eat clams."

Lynn helped get the messy, smelly clamshells into a big plastic bag.

"I'd better run over to the dump with that now," Grandmother said, "or Cyrano will get into it. It will only take a minute."

"I'll come with you."

The fog made Lynn nervous. Grandmother had to drive slowly with her head out the window and her lights on. They reached the dump safely, and Lynn threw the bag into the trash pit.

"I feel as if I'm flying on instruments," Grandmother said. She turned her face toward Lynn a second, laughing. Her cheeks were red from the damp cold and her eyes sparkled.

"Can't see your hand before your face," Grandmother muttered as she turned into her own yard.

"Well, we're safely home," Lynn said.

"Oh!" Grandmother jammed on the brakes, but it was too late. The bumper of the Buick slammed and scraped against metal. In the dimness just ahead of them stood a car.

Lynn had been thrown forward against the dash, but she wasn't hurt. "Are you all right?" she asked.

"I've done it now. They'll take my license away."

"You couldn't help it. What idiot parked here anyway, with no lights or anything?" Lynn got out of the car and went around to look at the damage. "It's just scraped a little paint, Grandmother. Nothing bad."

But Grandmother sat where she was.

"Go away, Cyrano." Lynn pushed him away from her. She opened the car door on Grandmother's side. "Come in the house. It's all right. Don't worry." She put her long arm around her grandmother's shoulders and helped her out. "Don't worry, Grandmother." She was angry with the person who had parked there in such a careless way, causing an accident that had spoiled the day, just when it was going so well. She led her grandmother to the kitchen. "Sit down. I'll make you some tea."

"We'd better see whose car it is," Grandmother said, but she sat down at the kitchen table.

There was a knock at the back door. Grandmother started.

"I'll get it," Lynn said.

A man and a woman Lynn didn't know stood in the doorway. The man had a forceful jaw and a smile that showed a lot of teeth. The woman, somewhat younger, wore a beautiful teal blue raincoat and her blonde hair looked as if she had just come from the hairdresser. She seemed not to have been touched by fog at all.

They stared at Lynn for a moment, and then the woman said brightly, "You must be the granddaughter." Although she didn't openly look Lynn over, Lynn felt her taking in the muddy sweater that she had not yet changed, and the pervasive fishy smell. She wished she could make herself invisible.

"We were around front, but we couldn't raise anybody," the man said, in a hearty voice, as if he were determined to treat the whole situation as normal.

Grandmother turned in her chair and slowly got up. "Oh, it's Mr. and Mrs. Small. This is my granddaughter. I'm afraid I ran into your car."

The bland expression on the man's face disappeared. "Ran into my car? I'd better look." He left abruptly.

"Oh, dear," Mrs. Small said. "How on earth did that happen? Our new car . . ." She shook her head. "I hate to say it, my dear Mrs. Linley, but I don't think you ought to be driving."

Lynn couldn't stand it. "It was right in the way," she said. "In the fog no one could see it there. And we didn't expect it."

Grandmother shook her head at Lynn. "I'm sorry. I'll pay for the damage, of course. Do come in." She stepped away from the table, and Mrs. Small got a good look at her. Muddy socks, rolled-up wet trousers, old sweater, stained and wet apron, dirty face, untidy hair. Mrs. Small gave a little gasp.

Grandmother put her hand to her hair. "I'm afraid I'm a sight. We've been clamming."

"Clamming!" She frowned and shook her head. "Mrs. Linley, you must not do these irrational things. You will harm yourself. And then we who care about you shall all feel so terribly responsible."

Grandmother pulled herself together. "No one need feel responsible for me, Mrs. Small," she said. "Lynn, put the kettle on. We'll make some coffee. Excuse me a moment. I'll wash up." She walked out of the kitchen with straight shoulders.

Mrs. Small watched her go. She turned toward Lynn, who was putting the water on the stove. "You must not allow it. But of course, you are just a child. Oh dear. One does wonder what her children are thinking of. I suppose they just don't realize. And leaving you here alone with her. It's so unfortunate."

Lynn bit her lip. If she said anything, she would say something rude. Better just get the coffee served and pray they wouldn't stay long.

Mr. Small came back. "Not too serious," he said. "It will need a paint job across the back."

"It's hardly scraped," Lynn said.

He gave her the kind of smile she hated, that said her remark wasn't worth answering. "Where did Mrs. Linley go?"

Lynn caught the little face his wife made at him. "Washing up, I believe. They have been clamming."

"Clamming! At her age? Oh dear, oh dear. Really, her children ought to be informed about the state of things." He looked at Lynn.

"What state of things?"

"Your grandmother's mind, you must realize, is not as sharp as it was."

"It seems sharp to me." Lynn struggled not to lose her temper. "She's one of the sharpest people I know."

"No sensible person would go clamming at her age. And in a fog like this."

"It wasn't foggy. We went out before daybreak. It was lovely."

"Before daybreak," Mrs. Small said. "When you can buy clams in town all ready shucked?"

Lynn looked at them in despair. How could you possibly explain to people like this the excitement, the fun, the darned hard work, the intense satisfaction that she and Grandmother had had that morning?

Grandmother came back, her face and hands washed, hair hastily combed, and the wet clothes exchanged for a blue and gray caftan that made her look regal. Lynn remembered the caftan. She had helped her mother pick it out last Christmas, at Jordan Marsh. Grandmother makes Mrs. Small look like a piker, Lynn said to herself.

"Please come into the sitting room," Grandmother said. "Lynn, will you pour the coffee? The fruitcake is already sliced."

"Oh, you mustn't bother for us," Mrs. Small said, but she went on into the living room.

"I'll tell Henry at the insurance agency about your car," Mrs. Linley said. "If you'll get an estimate for him."

Mr. Small smiled his world-encompassing smile, as if he were in the pulpit of a large church. "You sound very knowledgeable. Have you had many accidents?"

She looked at him sharply. "I never had one before in my life."

But Lynn knew he didn't believe that. She tried to concentrate on the coffee as the others left the kitchen, but her hands shook with anger. She dropped the top to the coffee pot and it rolled against the stove with a clatter. She reached up for the coffee cups and nearly dropped one of them, only catching it in time before it landed on the floor.

She got the fruitcake and arranged it on a plate. Should she give them little plates or could they use their saucers? Better do it right. She got some of Grandmother's bread and butter plates down, found the pewter sugar and creamer and arranged them on the tray. Her mother never let her do this kind of thing. If it were anybody but the Smalls, she could enjoy it. But they were hateful. They were the Enemy. She saw at once why Grandmother was afraid of them.

She managed to carry the tray into the sitting room without accident. Grandmother looked stiff and formal. Though there was still a smudge over one eye, her dignity was unassailable. Lynn was proud of her.

They were talking about the price of Thanksgiving turkeys. That seemed a safe subject. Lynn passed the cups of coffee that her grandmother gave her, and she offered the cake to the Smalls. Mr. Small took a piece, but Mrs. Small smiled her refusal and said she was watching her weight. She obviously didn't need to, it must be that she didn't like Grandmother's cake, Lynn thought. Well, tough luck for her. It was the best fruitcake in the world.

Mrs. Small began to talk about a Mrs. Bradshaw, who had cancer. "We're trying to get the poor soul into the hospital," she said, "but she hates to give up."

"Don't make her give up," Grandmother said.

"But she's all alone with that old man."

"But he's her husband. He loves her."

"Mrs. Linley," Mrs. Small said in an exasperated tone of voice, "the woman is terminal."

Grandmother straightened a little and looked hard at Mrs. Small. "We're all terminal," she said.

Mr. Small turned to Lynn. In his heavily playful way, he said, "You were a bad girl playing truant today."

Lynn looked at him blankly. "Truant?"

"You went clamming instead of going to school. Shame on you."

"It's Sunday," Grandmother said, and at almost the same moment Lynn said, "It's Saturday." Grandmother began to look rattled.

Again the significant glance between the Smalls.

"Oh, well," Mrs. Small said, "they aren't going to expel you for one day, I suppose. Whose room are you in?"

"I . . ." Lynn's throat seemed to freeze. "Will you have more cake?" She passed it to Mrs. Small.

"I haven't had any, dear. I'm dieting, remember?"

"You must be—what? Tenth grade? You're such a tall girl, it's hard to tell," said Mr. Small.

Lynn didn't know what she was going to do. But just at that awful moment, she was saved by a racket at the back door. Someone was banging on the door and shouting.

"Oh, what now?" Grandmother said. "I declare—"

"I'll get it," Lynn said quickly. She fled from the room.

She flung open the door and there in a swirl of fog stood Old Mitch with a plastic quart container in his hands. He stood on one foot, holding the other up as a crane might do, and stared at her.

"So that's who you are! Might have known. Family's full of thieves."

"What do you want?" she said as sternly as she could.

"Brought Miz Linley the first quart of scallops. She always buys my first quart. Where is she? I suppose you're Ella's girl. Mighta known. Can't trust any of 'em."

"She's busy." Lynn held out her hands for the container. "I'll give them to her."

"Want my money." He put out his hand to keep from falling. "Besides that, I scun my knee on somebody's bumper. Heck of a place to leave an automobile on a foggy day. Downright dangerous." He lifted his leg to show her his wound. The knee of his dirty old corduroy pants was torn, and there was blood on his leg. "Ought to sue."

"Oh, Lord," Lynn said. How could everything go so wrong. "You'd better come into the kitchen. I'll get a bandage or something."

He hopped into the kitchen and sat down heavily. "Likely to get blood poisoning. Danged rusty bumper. Whyn't she put her car in the garage where it belongs?"

"Because there was another one in the way," Lynn said sharply.

Her grandmother called from the other room. "What is the matter, Lynn?"

Before Lynn could answer, Old Mitch got up and hopped toward the living room. Lynn wanted to stop him, but it was impossible without actually tackling him.

He stopped in the doorway and surveyed the people. The Smalls looked startled and almost frightened. Old Mitch was quite a sight, Lynn thought, if you weren't used to him. Or even if you were.

"What do you want, Abner Mitchell?" Grandmother said calmly.

"Want my money."

"What money?"

"Scallop money. I brought the first quart, same as always. Ain't plannin' to cheat me out of my money, I hope."

"My granddaughter will get the money for you. In my purse in the kitchen drawer, Lynn."

"And what about my leg? Hurt my leg somethin' cruel on your car. It's sittin' there like a public nuisance." He thrust his knee close to Mrs. Small, who shrank back in her chair.

"Oh dear," said Grandmother. "I'm sorry about that, Abner. Come into the kitchen." She started to get up. "If you'll excuse me for a few minutes, I must see to Mr. Mitchell's knee."

"We must be going," said Mr. Small.

"I ought to have known," Old Mitch said, glaring at Lynn, "she was one of yourn. Swipin' livestock. Sashayin' around the island like a durned hippie. Why ain't she in school like a respectable girl?"

Grandmother looked at him sharply. "She is in school."

Lynn saw the attentive look on the faces of the Smalls. Her heart sank.

"I say she ain't."

"Stop talking nonsense, Abner, and come along while I fix your knee."

"You do go to school, don't you, dear?" Mrs. Small said sweetly.

"Of course, she does," Grandmother answered for her. "Let's don't have any trouble about that."

"Do you?" Mr. Small said to Lynn, smiling his fearful smile.

She saw what she had to do. They would say Grandmother was crazy, insisting that Lynn went to school when she didn't.

"I have not been going," she said in a clear voice, "but my grandmother doesn't know it."

She heard Grandmother gasp, but she didn't look her way.

Mr. Small looked as if he had just heard the loud crack of broken commandments. He said, "A truant child running wild on the island, yourself unable to take charge. . . . For your own sake and the sake of the child, steps must be taken, Mrs. Linley."

Old Mitch looked at Grandmother's face, and then he slewed around to face Mr. Small. "Steps? What steps?"

"It doesn't concern you, Mr. Mitchell."

"Don't concern me? You're threatenin' Miz Linley.

That concerns me. You folks are nothin' but off-islanders. You got no call to come buttin' into islanders' affairs." Forgetting his hurt knee, he took a step toward Mr. Small, who stepped back.

"We must get out of this crazy house," Mrs. Small said. She looked pale. "We're being threatened, Gerald."

"Threatened, are ya? And another thing. It was your automobile in the way of Miz Linley's that caused my accident. I may have to sue you." Mitch shook his fist.

"Abner," Grandmother said, "for pity's sake, be quiet and come into the kitchen."

There was a bang in the kitchen and a sudden patter, and Cyrano trotted into the room. He went directly to Mrs. Small and butted her gently in the stomach. She screamed. Grandmother sat down heavily. Old Mitch yelled with laughter.

"Lynn, remove the sheep," Grandmother said, in a voice of ice.

Lynn grabbed Cyrano, pulled him out of the room and shut him in the bathroom. "You're in disgrace," she said. "But it's nothing to what I'm in. I wish I were dead."

She heard the front door slam, and in a moment the sound of two cars starting up, as Grandmother moved her car so the Smalls could leave. Lynn went into the kitchen and found Old Mitch chuckling and eating a piece of fruitcake.

"I'm glad you're so happy," she said bitterly. "Now that you've ruined everything."

"Ruined?" His voice was full of pained surprise. "What kind of a way is that to talk? When I just stuck up for you? Told those snooty Americans where to get off."

"Oh, never mind," Lynn said. "How much are the scallops?"

Grandmother came into the kitchen. "I'll take care of it," she said to Lynn. "Get some water boiling, will you? I've got to clean up his knee. Roll up your pant leg, Abner." She didn't look at Lynn.

17 When Old Mitch had finally gone and the kitchen had been cleaned up in silence, Lynn made an effort to say something to Grandmother. She could think of no excuse that would sound reasonable, because she had always known her fears were not reasonable. Yet she couldn't bear the hurt, withdrawn look on Grandmother's face.

"Grandmother," she began.

Her grandmother hung up the dish towel. "Not now, Lynn. It's been a long day. I'd like a bath and a nap, I think." And she left the room.

Lynn looked at the clock. It had been a long day, all right—it seemed like weeks since they'd started out this morning. But it was only about one thirty. There was time to do something.

She ran upstairs, took a quick shower and dressed in her best wool dress and her good shoes. Then she went downstairs quietly and got her bike. There was a brief delay because Cyrano, who had been released from the bathroom by Grandmother, was determined to go with her. She finally had to shut him in the garage and ride away to the sound of his plaintive bleating.

Although the fog had thinned out a little, she had to be alert to keep from riding off the road. Once she was almost struck by a pickup that loomed up ahead of her.

She had worn her raincoat over her dress, but she could feel the hem of the dress getting wet as it flapped around her knees. She hoped it wouldn't shrink. Her hair was soaking wet, but it had been wet all day. She felt in her pocket to make sure she'd remembered her comb.

The best thing she could do was not to think about what she was going to say, and fortunately, the effort of keeping the bike on the road occupied her mind. Not just one day at a time, she thought, one minute at a time. If she thought about Grandmother, she would burst into tears right there on the foggy road.

She could have sworn it was Saturday. She had kept careful track of the days at first, but she must have grown careless. She stopped in front of the school and left her bike. With her hands clenched at her sides, she marched up the steps and into the office.

A secretary looked up. "Help you?"

"I'd like to see the principal, please." Her voice sounded as hoarse as a foghorn.

"What is it about?"

She hesitated, and a dozen misleading answers went through her mind. She almost said, "If he's busy, I can come in another time." But instead she said, "I want to enroll in the school. My name is Lynn Grenville."

The secretary looked interested. "Oh, yes. Mrs. Linley's granddaughter. Just a minute, Lynn. I'll see if he's busy."

Lynn groaned inwardly. They'd known all about her all along then. She'd be punished somehow. You couldn't just skip school for almost two months without anybody punishing you. Just so they let Grandmother alone. Poor Grandmother, who hadn't known a thing about it. Grandmother, who had trusted her. Her eyes filled with tears, and she had to scrub them hastily before the secretary came back. She hoped her whole appearance was so damp, the tears wouldn't show.

"This way, Lynn." The woman opened the gate built into the counter and led her to the office in back. "Mr. Tracy, this is Lynn Grenville." She moved away, and Lynn was left standing there.

The man stood up. He was about her father's age,

and he wore dark-framed glasses. That was all Lynn could see at the moment. "Hello," he said. "Sit down, won't you?"

She made herself walk to the chair by the desk and sit in it. As she put her hand on the arm, she noticed she still had mud under one fingernail. Hastily she withdrew her hand and covered it with the other one.

"What can I do for you?" he said.

Make me walk the plank, she thought. But she said, "I would like to go to school here, if that's all right with you."

"I see." He hadn't smiled, but he wasn't unpleasant. "What year of high school were you in on the mainland?"

"I'd be in the ninth."

He fiddled with some papers, and then pushed a pad and pen toward her. "Will you write down the name and address of your former school, so we can send for your records."

A ray of hope flashed through her head. "I won't be able to go to school till they come?" Maybe a week, or even two more weeks, of freedom.

But he said, "Oh, you can start Monday." He gave her some cards. "Will you fill these out and bring them in Monday morning, for our records. We'll work out your schedule then. We'll need Mrs. Linley's signature on the pink card. Your parents are in Europe, I believe?"

"Yes." If they knew all that, why hadn't they clamped down on her? Where was the truant officer? It was puzzling.

Then he said, "I just heard last week that you were here with your grandmother." That explained it. "I thought you would probably be in to see us." He consulted a chart. "You'll be in Mrs. Archer's room. That's . . . let's see . . ." He paused and then picked up his phone. "Miss Folger, I think Walter Patterson is in study hall. Would you ask him to come here a moment?" He hung up. "Walter Patterson is from the mainland and is a ninth-grader, too. He just came to us about a month ago. His father died suddenly."

"Oh," she said. "That's sad."

"Yes. He was a brilliant historian. Walter's mother's family were island people." He paused, and Lynn was sure he wished he could get rid of her and get back to work. She longed to ask him if the kids here were really so mean and tough, but for all she knew, he might be an islander himself. She cleared her throat.

"How is your grandmother?" he asked.

"Fine. She's just fine, thank you."

"I've met her once or twice. Fine-looking woman."

"Yes. Yes, she is. She certainly is." She felt like adding, "and she's not one bit kooky or off her rocker. If anybody is off her rocker, it's me." But she sat there, trying not to wriggle in her chair. She felt a sneeze coming, and she pressed her finger against her lip to stop it.

"Ah, here's Patterson." The principal looked relieved. "Patterson, I wonder if you'd show this young lady where Mrs. Archer's room is, where the lockers are, all that sort of thing. She'll be starting classes here on Monday. Since you're both mainlanders, I thought you could show her the ropes."

"Yes, sir."

Lynn turned around and caught her breath. It was Ishmael. He gave no sign of recognition. In fact, he hardly looked at her.

"You run along with Patterson, then, and we'll see you on Monday, Lynn."

She remembered to get up. "Yes. All right. Thank you very much."

With never a word to suggest he had seen her before, Walter Patterson took her on a quick tour of the building, showing her where her homeroom was, where the lockers were, the study hall, even the gym. They ended up at the front doors.

"Thanks," she said. It was a funny feeling to thank a ghost for showing you around your new school.

"That's okay." Then for the first time he looked directly at her. "If anybody hangs you out the window, let me know." And he was gone.

Lynn felt so relieved, she rode home at a reckless speed, once almost dumping herself in a patch of tall beach grass as she skidded around a fog-shrouded turn.

School couldn't be all that bad if she had a ghost to protect her. It wasn't until she was almost home that she remembered with a sinking heart that now she would have to face Grandmother and explain her deception.

18 Several implausible stories flitted through Lynn's mind as she stowed her bike away in the garage. She could say she hadn't been feeling well enough for school and she hadn't wanted to bother Grandmother about it. What would she have had? Fainting fits? Sore throat? Headaches? Maybe migraine headaches. No, that wouldn't do. She could say she'd understood she had to wait until her records came from the mainland and they hadn't come yet. But that wouldn't explain why she had pretended to be going to school. She could say. . . .

She walked into the kitchen and said, "Grandmother, I've been playing hooky, and I don't have any good excuse. I mean hooky every day. But I went to school just now and I enrolled. I start Monday." She let her breath out in a long sigh and waited.

Her grandmother was sitting on the kitchen stool reading *Phineas Redux*, and Cyrano was settled at her feet. She looked at Lynn over her glasses. Something that smelled like piccalilli was simmering on the stove.

Lynn couldn't bear Grandmother's searching look. "Cyrano," she said crossly, "who let you in?" She started to push him toward the door.

"Let him be," her grandmother said. "A lamb can get lonesome."

Lynn took off her raincoat and hung it up. She noticed that her best shoes were soaked and took them off. "I'm sorry about what I did." She put the school material on the table. "The principal wants you to sign this. If you don't mind." Her voice broke, and she began to cry.

"Come now," Grandmother said, putting her book-mark in the book and taking off her glasses. "No need to cry. You're damp enough without tears."

"I'm so sorry for what I did." Lynn struggled to get her weeping under control. What a baby she had been.

"It did take me by surprise. More like the kind of little trick your mother might have played on me. But I don't believe it was a trick. Something was the matter, wasn't it?"

"Yes. But it's so . . . I'm ashamed to tell you. It's so babyish. I hate myself."

"No, no, never hate yourself. That's like committing suicide. This is not an easy world to get through, some-times, but if you don't like yourself, that's a terrible handicap. Why don't you get out of that wet dress and come tell me about it? I'll just put the preserves on the back of the stove." She stepped over Cyrano and took the pot off the burner. "Put something warm on, Lynn. I think I'm coming down with a cold. It would never do for both of us to have one." She gave a little laugh. "What would Mrs. Small say to such incompetence?"

Lynn changed into her bathrobe, and when she came down, Grandmother had a fire going in the sitting room and a pot of tea ready. Cyrano had moved as close to the firescreen as he could get.

"You needn't think," Grandmother said to Cyrano, "that you're going to spend the winter in the house. That would really give people something to mutter about. But since we've all had a hard day, I thought we should be together." She sneezed.

"You *are* catching a cold."

"Tea will fix it. This is herb tea." She settled down on the sofa. "Now, I will tell you this: I was upset when I learned that you hadn't been going to school. Deception hurts me. I always told my children I could take flat-out disobedience a lot better than I could take being fooled. But I know you must have your side of the story. Why don't you tell me about it."

After a minute Lynn began to talk. She told Grandmother everything, the kids at home who teased her about her height and clumsiness, Timothy's irritation, her mother's impatience, the terror of facing a new school, the stories of the girls on the beach. She finished by saying, "I know, I'm a coward. But it all seemed so awful, so impossible. I hated deceiving you. You don't know how I hated it, and how afraid I was that somebody would spring it on you."

"As they did," Grandmother said.

"I could have died when Old Mitch said that."

"It's unfortunate he had to say it in front of the Smalls. But I suppose they would have found it out anyway. They seem to make me their business."

Lynn waited. She didn't know whether she was going to get a lecture or forgiveness. She waited and got neither. She said again. "You can't imagine how sorry I am."

Grandmother nodded. She was looking into the fire. "Yes, I can imagine. Are you going to be frightened now, when you start school?"

"I guess so, but not so much as I expected. That boy, Walter Patterson his name is, I think he'll kind of be my friend."

"I knew his grandparents," she said. "On his mother's side. They were Smiths. I believe the great-grandfather was a seafaring man."

"A whaler?"

"I don't know." Grandmother reached down and rubbed one of Cyrano's ears. Then she sneezed again and said, "Oh, bother."

Lynn hadn't told Grandmother about her odd con-

versation with Walter Patterson that foggy day on the
wharf. That was something she wanted to keep to herself. As long as she didn't tell it, she could think of it
as half real.

"I don't suppose," Grandmother said, "that island
children are any more formidable than mainland children. Of course islanders are very independent people
and they rear their children to be independent, too. But
I've never found that they were mean or cruel. At least
no more than anybody else, maybe a little less." She
swallowed and put her hand to her throat. "I seem to be
getting a sore throat."

Lynn persuaded her to go to bed. While she was
fixing some soup for her, she thought about the conversation they had just had. She had expected a scene or
a bawling out or something. But Grandmother didn't
seem to be wrought up about it one way or the other.
Still there could be trouble even yet. The Smalls had
been made to look foolish; Cyrano had frightened them
and Old Mitch had laughed. They weren't the kind of
people to forgive that.

She saw that Grandmother took some of the soup,
then went off and let her sleep. Before she, herself, went
to bed early because it had been a long, hard day, she
got a fresh pitcher of water for her grandmother. Her
grandmother looked feverish and Lynn touched her
forehead. It felt hot.

"Should I get a doctor?" she asked.

"No, no," Grandmother murmured. "Don't get one of those strange doctors in here. He'll bundle me off to the hospital or somewhere. They always do. I'll just sleep it off."

But Lynn lay awake a long time, even though she was terribly tired, worrying about Grandmother and feeling remorse for her sins.

19 This time it really was Saturday. Grandmother was still asleep, although Lynn could hear her cough now and then. She hoped her cold wasn't going to get bad. After she had checked on Cyrano and given him a slightly wizened bunch of carrots that Grandmother had said he could have, she put some water on to make coffee for Grandmother. She had never made it in this glass coffee pot that you used the filter papers with, but she read the directions on the filter box. Couldn't be simpler.

She poured orange juice for herself and put a glassful in the refrigerator. Maybe Grandmother would like breakfast in bed. She got a small tray, put a crocheted doily on it, and arranged coffee cup, plate, sugar and cream. Even heated up some coffee cake.

When she went to see if Grandmother was awake, she found her with eyes closed and decided not to disturb her. In the kitchen she drank her own orange juice and had some coffee cake. The day before still bothered her, but not quite so much. School was the same frightening unknown, but having Grandmother find out was over. And yet she would have felt better if Grandmother had really scolded her, punished her. Then she could have put it behind her. She still felt guilty. And she worried about the Smalls.

"Lynn?" Grandmother sounded faint and far away. Lynn hurried to her. "How do you feel?"

Grandmother made a face. "Just a pesky cold. I may spend the morning in bed. It isn't a school day, is it?"

"No, it's Saturday."

"Oh, yes, that plaguey Saturday that I seem bound to mislay." She sounded hoarse.

"Is your throat sore? Mother always gargles."

"Can't stand gargling. I gag."

Lynn got her breakfast and brought it to her.

"I haven't had breakfast in bed since your grandfather passed away." She looked pale. "Well, you know what those doctors say: bed rest and liquids, eight dollars please."

"Keep covered up, Grandmother."

"I will. You amuse yourself, now. If I need you, I'll sing out."

Lynn didn't know what to do with herself. She didn't want to leave the house, because Grandmother might want something, so she finally settled down in the living room with *The Compact Book of Waterfowl and Lowland Game Birds.*

Toward noon the phone rang. A woman, whom she thought was Mrs. Small, asked for Mrs. Linley.

"She's having a nap. Can I give her a message?"

"No, thank you, I'll call later."

"Who was it, Lynn?" Grandmother asked.

"She didn't say, but I think it was Mrs. Small. If she calls back, what shall I say?"

"Tell her I've gone clamming." Grandmother laughed and then had a fit of coughing. She shook her head. "Not really."

"I know. You ought to have some cough medicine."

"I'm all right. I'll rest awhile."

The second call came late in the afternoon. "Lynn, this is Louise Small. Is your grandmother all right?"

Lynn made her voice surprised. "Why, yes, she's fine, thank you. How are you?"

"Please tell her I'll be in touch. We're fine, thank you."

"I'll tell her." She found Grandmother awake. "Mrs. Small will be in touch."

"I have no doubt."

"She and Mr. Small are fine."

Grandmother made a face. "I'm so thankful."

Lynn laughed. It was fun sharing a secret enemy with Grandmother.

Grandmother coughed all night, and Lynn worried. In the morning she would go to the village and find either a doctor or that nice pharmacist.

Grandmother looked worn out in the morning. So Lynn got her breakfast and left for town. She rode as fast as she could, hating to leave her alone. During the night the fog horns had stopped their wail. The sky was gray, but the air was clear.

She parked her bike in front of the drugstore. Closed on Sunday. Of course it would be. Luckily there was a pencil in her pocket, so she wrote down the druggist's home number and called him from a pay phone.

"I'd need a prescription for anything that would do her any real good," he said. "Let's see, Dr. Fitz has gone sailing, John is out picking cranberries. . . . Say, that summer fella is here, that Dr. Ault."

"Oh, good," Lynn said. "I know him. I'll get him."

After racing home on her bike, she looked up his number and called. He answered the phone himself.

"My grandmother went clamming, and now she's got a terrible cough."

"Does she have her own doctor?"

"He died. She doesn't know the others."

"Will she put up with me?"

"Oh yes, I think so. She likes you."

"I'll be at the house in ten minutes."

She was waiting for him when he arrived and took him to her grandmother.

"Dr. Ault," Grandmother said. "Unexpected pleasure." She coughed for several minutes. "I'd be surprised to see you if I had enough strength left for surprise."

"Just so you're pleased," he said. "The surprise can keep. I want to thump your chest. The stethoscope I've got here is practically an antique, but I guess it'll do."

Lynn went out into the kitchen and worried. It seemed like a long, long time that the doctor was in Grandmother's room. She could hear a few murmured words, like "deep breath now," "in, out," "open your mouth and flatten your tongue." It made her so nervous she went into the living room where she couldn't hear him at all.

At last, he came out. He didn't look grave, the way doctors do on TV when the patient is in critical condition. "She's got a nasty chest cold," he said. "At her age we don't like that too much. I'm going to rouse Joe and get a couple of prescriptions filled. I'll bring 'em out to you. Meanwhile, keep her warm. Plenty of liquids." And he was gone.

Lynn went in to her grandmother, who looked drowsy. "Suppose he said plenty of liquids and bed rest," she murmured.

Lynn giggled. The relief of having Dr. Ault take charge made her feel weak in the knees. Grandmother's eyes closed, and Lynn left her alone.

She let Cyrano into the kitchen with her. "Tomorrow I start school," she told him. "And I haven't had time to be scared."

20 When Dr. Ault came back, he called Lynn into the room. Grandmother was sitting up. The doctor had just given her a shot, and he was holding out a glass of water and a tablet for her.

"Lynn, I want her to take one of these every four hours. And the cough syrup, one teaspoonful every two hours. I've written it down here."

"All right," Lynn said.

"Miss Haines, the district nurse, will check in in the morning when you're at school."

"I could stay home . . ." Lynn began.

"No," Grandmother said firmly.

"No, that isn't necessary." He looked at Grandmother. "Now look, Mrs. Linley . . ."

Grandmother glanced up at him in alarm. "You're going to say something unpleasant, otherwise you wouldn't say 'now look.' "

He laughed. "On the contrary. You'll thank me for it."

"If you think I'm going to any hospital or any kind of home for the senile, you're very much mistaken."

"You aren't sick enough for the hospital. They wouldn't take you. What do you mean about senile?"

"People around here think I'm ready for the geriatric ward."

He looked genuinely surprised. "You're kidding! Who?"

"Oh, well-intentioned citizens . . ."

". . . that can't leave people alone," Lynn finished. It had suddenly struck her that perhaps Dr. Ault could help. "They keep telling Grandmother she ought to be in a home."

Dr. Ault sat down on the edge of the bed. "Why?"

Grandmother sighed. "I'm forgetful. It's true. I forget things. I even forget who people are."

Dr. Ault touched her wrist. "Listen. My ten-year-old son has forgotten, for three weeks running, to bring home his torn catcher's mitt so I can tape it for him. He can't remember anything. But I'm not going to clap him into a Home for Forgetful Boys. At times our memories are not as good as they are at other times. That's not a problem; it's simply a fact."

"They're afraid I'll burn the house down or forget to eat my meals or something."

"My son is a lot likelier to burn a house down than

you are, I imagine. As for eating your meals, if you get really hungry, your stomach will remind you."

Grandmother smiled. "What a sensible young man you are."

"They can't make her go, can they?" Lynn asked. "They aren't even our family."

"Of course not. Not even the family could, unless they got doctors to declare her totally incompetent." He gazed at Grandmother. "And this lady is about as far as anybody can be from a situation like that."

Lynn still felt a little worry. "Would you sign something to say she's okay, if it was necessary?"

"Certainly. And that brings me to what I was going to say. I have to go back to Boston on the night boat, but now . . . wait, Mrs. Linley, hear me out. I have a friend who's new here, been here about four months. He was my roommate in med school. His name is Dr. Dan Cutter. I've talked to him about you. I'd like to suggest that you let him take over as your family doctor."

Grandmother frowned. "I am leery of strange doctors."

"He's not strange. He's a nice guy." He grinned at her. "A real swinger, like me."

"That sounds good, Grandmother," Lynn said. "He could keep the Smalls away."

"Oh, it's the Smalls, is it," Dr. Ault said. "Listen, don't

let the Smalls bug you. They're perfectly nice people—well-meaning and all—but they are kind of in the habit of running other people's lives, and they can't seem to quit. There's not a thing in the world they can do to you."

"They talk about social workers and homes and all," Grandmother said.

"I'll tell you what it is, Mrs. Linley; they're retired, and like a lot of retired people they don't know what to do with themselves. I'd call it a geriatric problem." He grinned at her again.

She laughed and had to wait for the coughing to stop before she answered him. "They're geriatric problems, are they?"

"Oh, classic cases." He patted the blankets that covered her knees and stood up. "So you'll let my friend Dan run interference for you, will you? I'd like to have him check that chest of yours tomorrow, if you don't mind."

"If he's not too busy," Grandmother said. "I don't suppose I'm dying."

"Not hardly. And Dr. Cutter is not all that busy. He wishes he were. Maybe you can recommend him. He's a heck of a good doctor, and he loves the island. I hope he can make it here."

"I'll do what I can. I don't see people much any more."

That was smart of Dr. Ault, Lynn thought, as she

walked to the door with him. Now Grandmother would see it as helping Dr. Ault's friend stay on the island, instead of the doctor caring for her.

"Thanks an awful lot," she said. "You've taken a big load off Grandmother's mind. And mine too."

He wrote down Dr. Cutter's phone number on his prescription pad. "I'll ask Dr. Cutter to come by to-morrow. If her temperature goes up or she seems to be wheezy, call him right away. She ought to be all right. I gave her an antibiotic. And don't let her worry. I know the school of thought that says an old lady living alone ought to go where people can look after her, but I don't go along with it unless it's really necessary. It's true she could fall and break her hip, or she could have a stroke, but all of us take chances like that every day. That doesn't mean we all have to have keepers. I've seen too many nice old people go right downhill once they had to give up their homes. Anyway she's got you."

"Yes, I'll be here a year anyway."

"Hey, you've got a sheep."

Cyrano came up to them with his lopsided gallop and nuzzled Lynn's hand.

"He's my pet."

He patted Cyrano. "That's great." He started to go and turned back. "You may have run into Dr. Cutter's girl at school. Her name's Lucy."

"No . . . not yet . . ." Lynn swallowed.

"She'll be glad to see another mainlander." He waved and ran down the walk to his car.

When Lynn came back to Grandmother's room, Grandmother said, "Well, isn't he a nice boy."

"Yes, he's great."

"I believe I feel a little stronger already. It must be that shot he gave me."

But Lynn thought it might be because now she didn't have to worry about the Home for Aged Women.

"I hope school will go well, Lynn."

"I'm not so scared as I was."

Grandmother slid down in the bed and closed her eyes. Lynn was about to tiptoe away when she spoke. "I was shy at your age."

"You?" Lynn could hardly believe it. Poised, cool Grandmother? It was true, she didn't see many people now. But that didn't make her shy.

"I crashed around like a young colt. And I blushed all the time."

"Me, too."

They were both silent for a while. Then Lynn picked up the copy of *Phineas Redux*, which had fallen to the floor, and put it where Grandmother could reach it when she felt up to reading. "If you'll tell me how to make clam chowder, I'll try my hand at it for dinner."

Grandmother smiled without opening her eyes. "Well, you take and steam a bunch of clams . . ."